D0735619

THE PASSENGER

DANIEL HURST

INKUBATOR
BOOKS

PROLOGUE

The sound of the body going underneath the train was heard by all of those inside the station that night.

A sickening combination of shattering bone and squealing brakes was not what most people were expecting to experience as they made their way along the platforms at the end of another long day.

Most people heard only the sound of the screams from fellow travellers as the desperate driver brought the train to a stop as quickly as possible, but there were a few who had been unlucky enough to see the incident itself. Those unfortunate souls would be going home with several distressing pictures flashing through their minds.

They would see the image of the man as he fell from the safety of the platform and down onto the hard track below. They would have the memory of the blood as it sprayed up the front of the train and across the windscreen in front of the startled driver. And it would be impossible to forget the looks of horror on the faces of their fellow witnesses who had all seen such a gruesome sight.

But there was one more thing that the eyewitnesses would recall about this terrible event.

They would recall the woman who had pushed that man in front of the train.

She had blonde hair and wore dark sunglasses. She displayed a calm expression while everyone around her wore one of shock. And she had hurried away while everybody else had stayed still.

There were many unforgettable things about that evening in the train station, and many questions for the witnesses, police, and paramedics to try to answer afterwards. Questions like:

Why did this happen?

Who was the unlucky man on the tracks?

And most important of all: *Who was the woman who pushed him?*

1

STRANGER

THREE HOURS EARLIER

There aren't many better spots to people-watch than at a London train station in rush hour. You get all kinds of people in a place like this. Young, old. Rich, poor. Happy, sad. *Mainly sad.* All of them buzzing about like little bees, desperate to get to their next destination as quickly as possible, and none of them caring about who they have to shoulder-barge out of the way to get there.

I could spend hours standing here and watching them all rush by, one, because I have the patience after spending so much time in prison, and two, because I find it fascinating. Everyone has their own story to tell, their own tales of love, regret and bad luck. But I don't have that much time to give to such a passive pursuit now. That's because there is one person in this crowd whom I have my eye on in particular: the brunette woman currently standing several yards to my left on this crowded platform.

There are dozens of people in between us, but I am making sure to keep my eyes on her more than anybody else. Unlike all these strangers whose life is still a mystery, this particular woman holds no secrets for me. I have been watching her for a while now, and I know everything about her, but importantly, she knows nothing about me.

Yet.

Her name is Amanda Abbott, and she is thirty-seven years old. She is from Brighton and lives in a two-bedroom flat near the town's train station with her seventeen-year-old daughter, Louise. Every weekday, Amanda catches the 07:40 train and makes the sixty-minute commute from the coast into London, where she works a nine-to-five office job as a purchasing administrator. Then she boards the 17:35 service back home again. If her weekday routine seems dreary, her weekend one is even worse. She spends most of it cooped up in her flat, leaving only for food shopping or a short walk along the windy seafront. Her love life is non-existent, and her social life seems just as scarce. From what I have gathered, this is not down to any lack of looks or social skills, but rather a dogged determination to use almost every spare minute she has outside of her employment to focus on her number one goal in life.

Amanda wants to be an author.

I haven't read any of Amanda's work yet, and I'm not planning on doing so. I don't need to know what she dreams up in her imagination every day. I only need to know what her reality is, and after the last few weeks, I have a pretty good idea of that. She's just an average woman, working an average job, dreaming of bigger and better things. I doubt she is any different from any of the other people standing between us on this platform right now. A commuter preparing for another commute.

How ordinary.

But there is one thing that makes Amanda stand out from this crowd. It's the thing that has kept me awake at night with excitement and anticipation of this day right here. It's the fact that unlike most sensible people in society, Amanda doesn't keep her money in a bank.

It's easy in my position at one of the busiest train stations in Central London to get pushed off course by a stream of rude passengers or be deafened by all the chatter, the public address system, and screeching of brakes as the locomotives go up and down the tracks. If I had to do this every day, then I'd probably kill myself, and I'm only slightly exaggerating. I'd definitely rather be back in prison, that's for sure. At least there I had some free will. Not like these people. They think they are free, but they are wrong. None of them want to be here, yet here they are, because they have to be. *Go to work. Go home. Do it all again tomorrow.* And they think they have a better life than an inmate. At least I had free accommodation and food. *I dread to think how much these guys are paying for the cost of living around these parts.*

Amanda is just like them. I can see that on her face as I maintain a visual on her while waiting for the 17:35 service to arrive. She looks bored. A little lost.

Sad.

She doesn't want to be here. She'd much rather be doing something else. But this is her life. Every decision she has made has led her to this moment right now. It's those decisions that have also led to a man like me being so interested in her. But there is still time for her to make one more decision. It will be a big one, and the outcome of it will have a significant impact on both her and her daughter. It's a decision she would never have expected to have to make. But she will make it.

She has no choice.

I notice Amanda turn her head in my direction, so I quickly avert my gaze from her pretty face and look down at the empty tracks in front of me. Soon a train will fill this space, but until then it's just a cavernous gap that only takes one push to send a person tumbling down into it. Sometimes the trains around here get delayed because there's a person on the tracks. But that doesn't mean somebody is playing around on them. It means they either jumped or they were pushed. A scary thought. Not one I'd like to entertain for long. But a thought that reminds me how fragile life is. The edge of this platform is literally a precipice between life and death.

I know which side I'd rather be on.

Looking up from the tracks again and back to my left, I see that Amanda is no longer looking in my direction. She doesn't know it yet, but it won't be long now until I'm the only thing she is looking at.

By the time we reach the end of this line, I will no longer be just a stranger in the crowd to her. She will know me almost as well as I know her. She will also have made that decision. I just hope she does the right thing. For my sake. For her daughter's. And for herself.

But there's only one way to find out.

We need to get on board.

Now, where is the train?

2

I stand on the same part of the platform that I stand on every day. I'm in the middle, not at the end because that part of the platform is exposed to the open air, and not at the beginning where the majority of commuters wait because they are too lazy to walk further than they have to.

The middle. My spot.

It's familiar. It's routine. It's my life.

But not for much longer.

I glance up at the digital screen hanging above the platform for an update on the service that is due to take me home tonight. The train should have been here by now, but there is no sign of it yet. The combination of digits and words on the screen tell me why. The 17:35 service from London Victoria to Brighton is now due at 17:44. A nine-minute delay. The train might come sooner, but it could be even later. Until then I'm stuck here with the hundreds of other people who just want to get home, put their feet up, and have a glass of wine.

It's frustrating. It's out of my control. It's not fair.

Welcome to my world.

The crowd swells around me as more and more commuters make their way through the ticket barrier and arrive on the platform. I watch them all jockeying for position as they attempt to get as close to the edge of the track as possible in anticipation of the train that will eventually arrive here.

The heat is stifling and not just because it's been a hot summer's day in the capital. It's because of all the extra body warmth around me right now. I really hope the air-conditioning is working on this train tonight. It failed on yesterday's journey home, and I was so sweaty by the time I got off in Brighton, I just about felt ready to throw myself into the sea. But I shouldn't complain. It's rare we get this kind of balmy weather here, and the way my finances have been over these last few years, the English sun is the only kind I get.

Somebody nudges me from behind, causing me to turn around and look at them. But they just stare back with no apology. I didn't expect one. This is London. But I'm not moving. I have my spot, and I'll be damned if anyone is going to push me out of it.

It's a sad indictment of how predictable my life is that I know exactly where a certain set of doors on the train will be when it arrives here. The doors to the fifth carriage will stop right in front of me—I've done this so many times that I have it down to an art form. While many of those around me will push and shove in their rush to get a seat when the train arrives, I will simply step right on and go to my usual seat because I have memorised the most efficient way to do this.

It's depressing that my life is this mundane, but you have to take the small victories when you can, and it's much better to have a good seat for the upcoming journey than be one of the people who end up standing in the aisles most of the way home. It will take an hour to get to Brighton from here, and that's a long time to be on your feet and clinging on to a handrail. It's much more comfortable to be seated if you can. But there are too many people here for everybody to get a seat, at least immediately. I guess it's just like anything else in life. Some will be lucky, and some will not. But I don't have to worry about that. I've been doing this for so long that luck doesn't even come into it.

I'll enter the fifth carriage efficiently when the train arrives, and I will rush to the set of two opposing seats with the table about halfway down. There, I will slide quickly into the forward-facing seat by the window before taking my laptop out of my bag and setting it up while the rest of the commuters rush around me for their own spots. I take that particular seat because it allows me to actually do something productive on my journey home.

By the time the train is leaving London, I will be in full flow.

While most people on this service will pass the time playing games on their phone, reading a newspaper or sleeping, I will get to work, typing several hundred more words of the book that I have been writing while I have been travelling up and down this line for the last three years. I need that table seat because I need to be able to get my laptop out and write. Otherwise, I won't be able to work, and if I can't work, I can't change my life. The words I type aren't just a way for me to pass the time on a boring commute. *They are the way I will escape this boring commute forever.*

I've always wanted to be a writer, but it has taken me until the age of thirty-seven to get serious about it. That is down to a combination of many things, including but not limited to bad luck, a lack of confidence, and the general unpredictability of life getting in the way. But now, after all this time, I am finally going after what I want, and nothing is going to stop me.

Nothing.

My ears prick up as the station announcer comes over the tannoy to give an update on the delayed service.

'We are sorry to announce that the 17:35 service to Brighton is delayed by approximately twelve minutes.'

There are a few groans and moans from the people around me as the tannoy clicks off, and I look up at the screen to see that the estimated time of arrival has now moved on to 17:47. *Brilliant.* Every minute we are stuck here is one minute less we get to enjoy of our evening. But unlike the passengers around me, who are shaking their heads and muttering expletives under their breath, I at least have something to feel fortunate about.

I won't be standing here next week. I won't be forced to go through this tedious routine anymore. I won't have my life dictated to me by a station announcer. That's because I have handed my notice in at work, and I only have two more days left until I am a free woman.

The rush of exhilaration that accompanies that thought is only tempered slightly by the anxiety that comes with knowing that I won't have a stable income any longer. But I have to believe in myself, and I am sure I am doing the right thing.

I am positive that I am going to be able to make my dreams come true.

As I stare down at the tracks in front of me, I think about how my life is going to change in the coming days. After Friday, I will no longer be required to come into London and sit at a desk in an office to work for somebody else. Nor will I be forced to endure two hours of train rides every day along this line, a privilege that costs me a considerable chunk of money to experience.

That's because I am going to give my writing my full attention. I have been working hard over the last year, saving every penny I could to give myself this chance, and now it is time to do it.

It's time to see if all the writing, dreaming and sacrifices have been worth it.

My plan after leaving my job is to finish my book and then try to get it published. With the money I have saved away, I estimate I have at least a year or two to do this before my funds run out. I pray that it is enough time for somebody to pay me for my writing and save me from having to return to this nine-to-five life.

Am I confident? Yes.

Do I believe in myself? I wouldn't be doing it if I didn't.

But am I also afraid that I am making a mistake and will end up penniless?

Hell yeah.

I swallow hard as if to keep that knot of anxiety down in my stomach and remind myself that I am doing the right thing. What other choice do I have? Stay in my job and keep catching this train every day for the rest of my life? The thought of that terrifies me far more than the thought of failing. I know I can do it. I have to stay positive. My writing is good. Somebody will like it. Somebody will buy it.

I won't end up homeless at the end of it all.

But I know my fears are only made worse because it's not just me I have to worry about. It's my daughter too. Louise is seventeen, and she lives with me in our small flat in Brighton. While I have the money to pay the rent now, that might not be the case in the future if my book doesn't take off. Therefore, it won't just be me who ends up screwed.

It will be my child too.

I wish the damn train were here. I wouldn't be getting this worried if it was. That's because I'd be too busy writing to even think about the fear of failure. But as it is, I'm still stuck here on this platform, and my overactive imagination is running away with itself.

I know I am taking a risk. I know it's not just my life that could be ruined if it doesn't work. Louise could have hers ruined too.

That explains why she doesn't agree with what I am doing.

I reach into my handbag and take out my mobile phone, deciding at that moment to give my daughter a call to do something nice for her. I'm going to ask her if she would like a takeaway tonight. That will earn me a few brownie points. It won't be a big thing, but an Indian or a Chinese will go a little way to keeping things civil between us, at least for one night anyway.

I unlock my phone and navigate towards my daughter's number and notice the wallpaper on my device. It's the one I saved as a way to motivate myself every day whenever I look at my mobile. It's a photo of a sandy beach in the Caribbean along with an inspirational quote typed across the clear blue sky: *"Dreams only work if you do."*

I saved that wallpaper to my phone a couple of years ago after a particularly hellish commute left me needing a little lift, and it always makes me feel good when I see it, even if it is a little cheesy. That tropical beach is certainly a long way away from this crowded platform in Central London, but I guess it wouldn't be a dream if it were real.

I tap my finger on the number on the screen and then hold the phone to my ear as I wait for my daughter to pick up. She will be at home now, most likely lying on the sofa and watching TV, because that's all she has done ever since she finished school last year and told me she didn't want to go to college. I wasn't too disappointed about her lack of interest in further education because I'm all for people doing whatever they want to do, and my daughter clearly did not want to sit in any more lessons. But the problem is, she isn't doing anything at all right now. She doesn't have a job, and she doesn't have a dream, other than to go travelling, which I am fully behind, but she needs to earn money before such a thing can happen. Louise talks about exploring far-flung continents like Asia or South America, but she doesn't seem to recognise that in order to fund those adventures, she needs to put in the work in less glamourous locations.

She can't hope to lie on a beach in Brazil if she doesn't make any money in Brighton.

Of course, Louise's answer to that is that I should just give her the money she needs to go. She knows I have been saving up, and she expects me to just give her a big chunk of that so she can jet off and enjoy herself while I keep working. But I've explained to her that life isn't as simple as that. If you want something, then you have to work for it yourself. Unfortunately, Louise doesn't seem to want to work for anything. But she won't have much choice for long. I'm going to give her a deadline to find a job. I don't care what it is. I can't have her sitting around at the flat all day, wasting her life, as well as my hard-earned money.

As the call connects and I hear my daughter's voice on the other end of the line, I say a silent prayer to myself in the hope that this conversation won't end up in yet another argument between the two of us.

But I'm not holding my breath.

3

LOUISE

'What?'

Most people answer the phone with friendlier words than that, but I don't because it's only my mum calling. Why would I bother to be polite when she is probably just ringing to give me another lecture on why I should be doing more with my day than sitting around the flat?

She thinks I'm lazy and barely move from my bed to the sofa in all the time she is at work. But she is wrong. I'm not lazy, and I do more than just hang around sleeping and watching television. I have so much more going on in my life than she realises, and the fact that I can't be honest and tell her that only proves to me how rubbish a parent she really is.

'How was your day?'

I can only just hear my mum's voice over the line through all the background noise around her. It sounds like she is at the train station, and it seems busy there, but I can still make out the weariness to her speech. She always sounds tired because she always is. She gets up early to go to London, and she gets back late. *What a life.*

Is it any wonder I'm not in a rush to follow her into the world of work?

'Fine,' I reply.

'What have you been up to?'

'Not much.'

I'm making sure to keep my answers short so this conversation doesn't go on any longer than it needs to.

'Please don't tell me you've been watching TV all day again. We talked about this,' Mum says, and I roll my eyes.

'I haven't. I spent a delightful ten minutes in the bathroom having a shower. Happy now?'

'Lou, you promised me you were going to apply for jobs today.'

I sigh because I can't be bothered to explain myself again. I only told her I would apply for jobs to shut her up last night when she was on my case. Of course I haven't applied for any. Why would I? She knows what I want to do. I want to go travelling. I'm seventeen. These should be the best years of my life. Yet my mum wants me to waste them making minimum wage in some poxy job. That might be what she did with her youth, but I'm determined not to go down the same path.

'Sorry for not wanting to be miserable like you,' I reply, and I don't even feel bad for saying that. My mum hates her life, and she's always in a bad mood. It annoys me that she thinks the right thing for me to do is become just like her.

'I'm not miserable. I just want the best for you.'

'No, you want the best for yourself. Otherwise, you wouldn't be following your dream and stomping all over mine.'

There, I've said it, and now here we are again. Less than a minute into our conversation and we're back having the same old argument. But I don't care. I want to make my mum feel bad about what she is doing because I feel bad about it. As long as I am unhappy, then I will keep reminding her why.

'Don't be ridiculous. I'm not stomping on your dream.'

'Yes, you are. You have the money to give me so I can go travelling, but you're quitting your job and spending that money on your stupid writing instead.'

I'm trying to stay calm, but I get frustrated when I think about how selfish Mum is being. She's giving up her job in London and putting our future at risk all because she thinks she can be a full-time author.

And she has the cheek to call me lazy.

'I'm not having this argument again,' Mum says as I hear a loud voice come over the tannoy at her end of the line. 'I just called to ask if you wanted a takeaway for dinner tonight.'

'Shouldn't you be saving your money for yourself?' I reply, my voice dripping with disdain.

'Louise, come on. I'm trying to do something nice here.'

'No, you're not. You're just trying to make up for being a crap mum. But it'll take more than a takeaway to do that.'

'Don't be like this. What do you fancy? We don't have to have a takeaway. We could do something else. Go out somewhere maybe?'

'Why are you bothering to ask me? Do whatever you want. You always do anyway.'

I hang up the phone, and it's a relief not to have to hear my mum's voice and that noisy train station anymore. For now, things are quiet and calm again. At least they will be until she gets home in an hour's time.

'Everything okay?'

I turn to look at the man lying beside me in my bed, and I smile. Thank God for my boyfriend, James. He's the only good thing in my life right now.

'Mum's just being a bitch again,' I tell him as I drop my phone on the bedside table and snuggle back down under the duvet with him.

'What did she say?'

'She asked if I wanted a takeaway.'

'Wow, what a bitch.'

I laugh and slap James playfully on the arm. 'That's not what I mean. She's just always on at me to get a job. I'm sick of it.'

James gives me a kiss on the head because he knows that will soothe me before speaking again. 'Try not to let her stress you out. And never mind that, what takeaway are we having? I'm starving.'

I smile at my boyfriend because he always makes light of things. He's just what I need to combat my mum, who only ever seems to bring me down.

'No takeaway for you. Not with your allergies.'

'That's not kind!'

I laugh because it's my nature to sometimes joke about things that scare me, and having a boyfriend who is severely allergic to peanuts is definitely one of those things.

'I'm only teasing. But you know you can't stay for dinner. You need to get out of here before she gets back.'

'Are you sure? I was thinking tonight would be a good time for me to finally meet her.'

'There is no good time for you to meet her. Trust me.'

I pull back the duvet to show James that I am serious about him getting up and leaving the flat before my mum comes back, but he reaches out and pulls it back over us.

'But I'm so warm under here. You wouldn't kick me out onto those cold streets, would you?'

'Cold? It's the middle of summer!'

'But it's still not as warm as in here.'

'That might be so, but I'd rather kick you out myself than have my mum do it for me. Seriously, she would kill me if she knew you'd been coming around here while she was at work.'

'I'm just your dirty little secret, aren't I?' James says, feigning disappointment. 'I feel so used.'

I laugh at my boyfriend's sense of humour again and really wish he didn't have to leave, but I'm not joking when I say that my mum would kill me if she found him here. It's not just the fact that she has no idea I have a boyfriend that would get me in trouble. It's also because of the age difference between us.

James is twenty-two, and while I don't care about the five-year gap, Mum most certainly will. She'll say he's too old for me, and she'll also say I'm too young to be having sex with anybody, let alone a guy I'm falling in love with. But she's wrong. James and I have been seeing each other for a month, and we are careful. This is nothing like when Mum was nineteen and got pregnant with me after a one-night stand. Unlike her, I'm actually taking precautions because I don't want to mess up my life by having a baby before it's even got going.

'You'll get over it. Now come on, get up,' I order James as I climb out of bed and pick up an old T-shirt from my bedroom floor and pull it over my head quickly. I'm not self-conscious of my body while I'm under the duvet with James, but I'm certainly self-conscious of it once I'm out in the open again.

'Your mum can't be that bad. I bet I could charm her into liking me,' James says as he puts his hands behind his head and watches me get dressed.

'No chance. She hates all men these days, not just the ones I'm seeing.'

'How many are you seeing?'

I pull my face. 'You know what I mean.'

James gives me a wink, and I wish I could be as relaxed about life as he is. He never seems to have a care in the world, whereas I constantly feel like I am never more than five minutes away from another stressful situation. But things have got better for me since I met him four weeks ago.

We matched on a dating app and had our first date on Brighton Pier, where we had a fun time playing in the penny arcades and throwing our chips to the seagulls as they flew past. But while the activities on the date might have seemed childish, the conversation certainly wasn't. I like the fact that James is older because he has a confidence about him that guys my age don't have. He seems to be comfortable in his own skin and untroubled by the prospect of the future, which is the exact opposite of me. I guess that's why I feel so good when I am around him.

That and the fact he is gorgeous.

'You don't seem to be getting ready to leave,' I say as I pick up my hairbrush from the dresser table and run it through my dark locks.

'Your mum won't be back for ages yet.'

'She'll be back in an hour, so move it.'

I see the reflection of James in my mirror and notice that he isn't getting up, and while there is still plenty of time for him to go yet, I'm starting to regret letting him come into the flat this late in the day. He usually comes around in the mornings when there is no chance of us getting caught together, but today he just randomly showed up in the middle of the afternoon, saying that he was desperate to see me. I was happy with the surprising show of affection, so I was willing to let him inside, but now I'm starting to get a little anxious. I know Mum's train always gets in around half six, and we aren't far from the station. If she walks in and he is still here, then it won't just be him getting kicked out.

It'll be me too.

'Are things really that bad between you?' James asks as I continue to brush my hair.

'Oh, yeah. We pretty much hate the sight of each other at this point.'

'Why?'

'Too many reasons to go into. Just trust me when I say that the sooner I get out of here, the better.'

'It can't be that bad,' James replies, a little too casually for my liking. 'Everyone hates their mum when they're a teenager.'

I stop and place my brush back on the dresser table. I haven't really gone into the full story of why my mum and I aren't as close as we could be with him before, but we are starting to get serious now, so maybe it is time.

I turn to face James and take a deep breath. He's already proven that he is more capable of handling an adult conversation than any of the guys my age, but this will be the biggest test of that yet.

'We had a massive argument a few months ago,' I say, thinking back to that dreadful night. 'It was horrible. We both said some nasty things. But then Mum said the worst thing. She basically admitted to me that I had been a mistake.'

'Ouch. She actually said that?'

'Not in those exact words, but I could tell she was alluding to it. She was blaming not being a full-time writer already on the fact that I came along when she was young and forced her into getting a different job so she could look after me.'

James says nothing for a moment, and I worry I've confessed too much. We've gotten serious pretty fast over the last month, but maybe this is a little too deep even for us. But then he speaks again and shows that he is mature enough to handle this topic.

'Wow. I knew things weren't great, but I didn't know they were that bad.'

'Yeah,' I say, shrugging my shoulders. 'And it got worse after she said that. I said I blamed her for not knowing who my father is. I accused her of sleeping around.'

'Ouch,' James says, wincing, and the look on his face confirms what I already knew. I went too far with what I said to Mum. But then again, she went too far with what she said to me.

I feel a little teary as I recall that awful night a year ago, and James must be able to tell because he finally gets out of bed and comes over to join me by the dresser table.

'I'm so sorry,' he says as he brings me in for a hug.

I feel the strength of his arms around me, and it makes me feel much better, although I know it is only fleeting. I really wish he didn't have to leave. I wish he could stay here with me all night and I could wake up to him telling me he loves me instead of my mum just telling me to get out of bed.

'No wonder you want to go travelling,' he says. 'I'm surprised your mum just doesn't give you the money for a flight. It sounds like she'd be happy for the space too.'

'That would mean less money for what she wants to do,' I reply, shaking my head. 'She's made it clear she isn't willing to make any more sacrifices now.'

I wipe my eyes as James lowers his arms and sits down on the edge of the bed. I really want to know what he is thinking, but I'm surprised when I actually find out.

'If only you knew the combination to that safe of hers. We could just take her money and run away together,' he says.

I'm surprised by that comment because I wasn't expecting him to even remember about that. He's referring to the safe in my mum's room that I told him about three weeks ago while we were lying in bed together.

The safe with all my mum's savings in it.

Mum's told me there are thousands of pounds in there, and I naively thought that meant she was saving up to give me a big chunk of it. Then she told me she was quitting her job, and I realised what she was really planning to use that money for. I've never known the code to that safe, but that hasn't stopped me from trying to access it before. Unfortunately, I could never get in, so she still has all the cash, and I'm completely broke.

'Yeah, it's a shame I can't open it,' I reply as I turn back to the dresser table and pick up the comb again. 'If only life were that easy.'

4

That phone call went about as well as I expected it to. I only rang my daughter to find out what she fancied for dinner, yet it turned into another argument, just like it always does. I don't know why I bother sometimes. I honestly thought trying to make it as a writer was the hardest job in the world, but it's easy compared to being a parent.

Writing can mean years of rejection.

Being a mum can mean a lifetime of it.

But it's not all bad news because I can see my train slowly making its way into the station towards me. Better late than never, I suppose. But because of the fourteen-minute delay, the commuter count on the platform has grown unbearably large, and I can see the station employees keeping even more passengers back behind the ticket barriers to prevent overcrowding. I'm still in my prime position at the front of the platform where the doors will open, but it's getting harder to keep my spot, and it's only going to get worse as the train comes closer and people become more desperate to score an elusive seat.

I clutch the strap of the laptop bag that is slung over my shoulder as another errant elbow digs into me from behind, but I don't bother to turn around this time because I know what I'll see. It'll be a flustered face belonging to a tired man or woman just as fed up about being here as I am. I know that he or she will be running entirely on the caffeine they used to start their day while dreaming about the alcohol they will use to end it.

Some in the nine-to-five world use ambition to keep themselves going, but most just use legal drugs.

The front of the train moves past me as it comes along the platform, and I catch a glimpse of the driver sitting inside at the controls as it does. He looks as thrilled with the delay as his passengers are. Finally, the train comes to a stop, and just as I knew they would be, the doors to the fifth carriage are now right in front of me.

There's a brief moment that all commuters will know as "the calm before the storm" until the doors unlock and slide open automatically.

That's when all hell breaks loose.

Everybody on the platform surges forward to the open doors, and it's only the fact that I am already wedged in so tightly amongst the bodies around me that prevents me from being knocked to the floor.

I step forward into the carriage but am immediately shoulder-barged to the side as a bulky businessman carrying a briefcase proceeds to bundle me out of the way in a sneaky bid to beat me on. But I'm no novice when it comes to this thirty-second dash, and I make sure to barge him right back before carrying on with my own scramble for a seat.

I'm grateful for the cool blast of air that I feel as I make my way deeper into the carriage. The air-con is working tonight, thank God. But that's about all I have to be grateful for right now.

There are many things in life that give hope to the human race, like random acts of kindness and generosity, or a cute dog being reunited with its owner after a long time, but there aren't many things that could extinguish that hope as quickly as witnessing the events on a commuter train in a city centre at rush hour. If an alien landed now and saw the scenes on this train, they would think that human life was just one big selfish scramble.

They wouldn't be far wrong.

I grit my teeth as I weave my way through the sea of shoulders, elbows, and huffing and puffing and keep my eyes focused on my usual seat in the carriage.

It's still available. I'm going to make it.

It's mine.

It's a relief to reach my traditional seat that is part of a two-seat set on either side of a table, but I still have to work fast to get myself sorted before the train departs. Quickly removing my laptop bag from my shoulder, I place it onto the empty table while noticing the attractive man arriving at the vacant seat opposite me. He gives me a brief smile as he removes his smart suit jacket before sitting down to get out of the way of the other passengers trying to squeeze past in the busy aisle.

I'm just about to do the same when a young woman comes out of nowhere and swoops in beside me, taking the seat I had already claimed as my own and leaving me standing without one.

'Hey!' I say to the annoyingly pretty female who has just broken one of the unwritten rules of train travel.

You don't get into a seat that somebody is preparing to sit down in. As public transport rules go, it's up there with "don't listen to loud music without headphones" and "try to avoid eating anything fishy". But the young woman doesn't even acknowledge what she has done and instead settles into the seat even more.

I'm furious. I'm tired. Most of all, I'm sick of putting up with this awful routine. And I'm just about to let this rude person know it. That is until the guy sitting opposite decides to do it for me.

'That's not cool,' he says, shaking his head. 'I'm sure your parents didn't bring you up to be that rude.'

The young woman frowns as if to say "Are you talking to me?" so the man makes it clear that he is.

'Yes, I'm talking to you. This lady here was just about to sit down. As you can see, she had already placed her laptop bag on the table, and she was in the process of removing her coat when you snuck in and stole that seat away from her. I think you should apologise and go and find another place to sit.'

I notice the young woman seems as surprised about this man's intervention as I am.

'Why do you care?' the woman scoffs back, and for a second I'm reminded of Louise. It makes me feel a little better to know that it's not just my daughter who has a bad attitude towards others.

'I care because she is my wife, and she is pregnant,' the man says, and now I'm even more surprised. 'I don't think it's fair that you are going to make her stand up all the way back to Brighton just so you can put your feet up. What are you? Eighteen? Nineteen? Come on, you've got the energy to stand.'

I'm not sure who this guy is and why he is pretending we are married or that I'm pregnant, but before I can question it, I see the young woman in my seat look at me with a sympathetic expression.

'I'm sorry. My bad,' she says, and she gets up and

scurries away down the carriage on the hunt for some-where else to sit.

Wow. I'm amazed.

That actually worked.

But I don't waste too much time thinking about it and quickly slump down into the vacant seat before anybody else can swoop in.

'Thanks, hubs,' I say jokingly to the man sitting opposite me, but he waves his hand in the air as if it was no big deal.

'Sorry for the whole marriage and pregnancy thing. I just knew that was the best chance to get her to give the seat back.'

I smile but also feel a little self-conscious. Does he think I could pass for a woman who looks pregnant?

My stomach isn't exactly flat, but I wasn't aware it was round.

'And I don't mean you look pregnant either,' the stranger quickly adds, and I laugh in relief.

'That's good to know. Thank you.'

We share a brief smile before the various noises in this chaotic carriage divert our attention away. Hurried chatter. Tannoy announcements. Arguing. Music. The rustle of a packet of crisps. The clatter of a suitcase on the floor. *It's like an orchestra of the mundane.*

I'm tempted to try to keep the conversation going with the stranger opposite me, if only because it's been a while since I got chatting with a good-looking guy, but the presence of the laptop bag on the table between us reminds me why I shouldn't. I am supposed to be working now. This is my golden hour. That one sliver of precious time in my day when I get to do what I really want to do instead of what I'm paid to do or what I'm obligated to do. My boss in the office cares little for my dreams of being an author, and my daughter cares even less, but I care, and that is all that matters.

But that book won't write itself.

With that in mind, I unzip the bag and slide out my silver laptop before lifting up the screen and pushing the power button. It's not the best computer on the market, and it takes an age to load up, but it was affordable, and it does what I need it to do, which is basically stay powered long enough for me to punch some words into it before it dies.

As I watch the screen run through its tediously long powering-up phase, I look around the carriage, and as expected, all the seats are now taken. I can see several people standing in the area by the doors, squeezed in almost as tightly as they were out on the platform, and I feel sorry that they are the unlucky ones today who won't get to sit down until we are well outside London.

And to think they are all paying good money for this.

But I can't let other people's problems distract me from my own, so I return my focus to my laptop, where I enter my eight-digit password, and now I am in.

There's no stopping me now. I can work all the way home. All I need to do is start typing.

'Wow, and I thought I was a workaholic.'

I glance up at the man sitting opposite me.

'Sorry?'

He gestures to the laptop between us. 'I thought the working day was over, but I guess you are proving me wrong.'

'Oh, this isn't work,' I reply with a smile, and I expect him to leave it at that. But I kind of hope he doesn't.

'What is it?' he asks me as he unfastens the top button on his white shirt and loosens his smart navy tie a little.

Hmmm, he really is good looking. I estimate that he is around thirty years of age, which is much too young for me of course, but then it feels like most people are these days. I've already begun my doomed descent into middle age, and now I feel as if anyone under the age of thirty-five possesses some elixir of youth that has somehow passed me by.

'What, this?' I say, gesturing at my laptop and trying to keep it casual. 'It's nothing. Just something I do to pass the time to Brighton.'

But the handsome stranger doesn't take that for an answer. 'Seriously, what are you working on there?'

I pause before telling him, not because I'm embarrassed about what I'm trying to achieve with my book but more because I know that mentioning it could lead to a long conversation. While I might like that based on his good looks, I don't really have the time for it. I should be writing already because it won't be long until I'm back at the flat and walking on eggshells around Louise again, but I know if I tell him I'm writing a book, then he will keep asking me about it or, worse, tell me he is writing his own.

It's amazing how many people turn out to be budding authors when they find out somebody else is working on a book. The last thing I need here is a repeat of my commute last Tuesday. I told the woman opposite me that I was writing, and she then spent the whole journey telling me about how she really needed to put her life story into print because she was certain that her book of memoirs would become a bestseller. Maybe it would, maybe it wouldn't, but either way, it wouldn't help me. I need to focus on getting my own bestseller, or I'll be riding this train until eternity.

But I still haven't answered his question.

Making a snap decision to avoid a lengthy conversation, I click the programme on my desktop that opens a game of *Virtual Solitaire* on my screen and turn it around to show him.

'See, nothing exciting. Just a game.'

The man smiles, and while I'm not exactly sure he buys it, I've at least saved myself from talking about my book for the next hour.

Instead, I'm free to actually write the damn thing.

'Ladies and gentlemen, we apologise for the delay to your 17:35 service to Brighton. This was due to a signal failure in Croydon, but that has been resolved now, so we will be on our way shortly. Estimated arrival time in Brighton this evening is now 18:53.'

Several more moans and groans spring up from the passengers around the carriage after the announcement from the driver. That's because it is confirmation that we will all definitely be late getting home tonight. But we knew that anyway after such a long delay, so I'm not sure why they are moaning now.

But never mind about that. The train starts to pull away from the station, and we're on our way. More importantly, my fingers are flying across my keyboard, and the words are pouring out of me.

This journey is going to absolutely fly by now.

5

STRANGER

I watch the woman sitting opposite me as she types furiously away on her laptop, and smirk to myself because it's the most unusual way to play solitaire that I ever saw. But I know she isn't really playing that game. I know exactly what she is doing. Of course I do. I know everything about her.

In a show of pathetic predictability, Amanda rushed to her usual seat on the train, and now she is working on her book, which is why her fingers are hitting her laptop keyboard as if her life depended on it. This is the closest I have ever been to her since I began following her, but I haven't been surprised by anything I have seen so far since we boarded this train. I already know she is very single-minded when it comes to the pursuit of her goal and has no time for men right now, and she just proved that when she made no attempt to keep the conversation with me flowing a moment ago. But that's okay. My feelings aren't hurt too badly.

We'll be chatting again soon enough.

As I keep my eyes on the focused woman before me, I can't help but admire her discipline and forward planning. It takes a lot of things to give up a stable job for something less reliable.

Confidence. Ambition. Courage.

But most of all: *money.*

While I suspect Amanda possesses those first three things, it's the fourth one that I am absolutely certain she does. Amanda definitely has money, around £20,000 I'm led to believe, and all of it locked away in a safe in the bedroom of her flat in Brighton. No wonder she is so willing to walk away from her job with that much cash to hand. I imagine a disciplined woman like her could make those funds last a long time while she pursues her ambitions in the writing world.

Too bad I'm going to take it all from her before she gets the chance.

I loosen my tie a little further, but I'm desperate to just take the damn thing off if I'm honest, along with this tight-fitting shirt and these ridiculous pin-striped suit trousers. I'm much more comfortable in jeans and an old T-shirt, and it won't be long until I'm back in my normal attire, but for now, I have to keep up appearances. I want Amanda to think that I am just like her and everybody else on this train.

Just another lowly worker making his way home after the grind of a day in the office.

My suit might look sharp on me, but it's nothing more than a cheap cut I picked up at a knock-down price in some lousy discount store in Brixton. Everything I'm wearing is second-hand, including the gold watch on my wrist, which I took from the guy I mugged in Vauxhall last week. The watch still remains from my haul that night, but I've spent most of the money from that man's wallet, which means I'm in need of more funds and fast. But I'm not just after some short-term cash today to tide me over until my next mark. What

I'm after this evening is a proper payday, and the woman sitting opposite me is going to be the one who gives it to me.

But I must be patient and bide my time. The train has barely left London, and it's still extremely busy. I need to give it ten minutes or so until we have left the capital behind and passed through a couple of stations before I make my move. The quieter the train is, the better. I don't expect Amanda will make a scene, not when I tell her what is at stake, but I still have to take my time and get this right. I can't afford to screw this up and not just because I need the money.

I can't afford it because I don't want to end up back in prison again.

I sit forward suddenly in my seat and take out my mobile phone from my trouser pocket, pushing the negative thoughts of potential failure from my mind and instead focusing on the task at hand. Amanda is busy working away on her own dream, so I should be doing the same.

Moving my fingers across the keypad on my phone's screen just as efficiently as Amanda's own hands on her laptop keyboard, I type out the message to my accomplice that will keep him up to date with the situation at hand.

"Train is late leaving London. New arrival time - 18:53."

6

'Get up! We're running out of time!'

I hear the frustrated plea from my girl-friend from the bathroom but remain in the same position I have been for the last ten minutes, which is under the duvet with my head resting on the pillow.

I'm in Louise's bed, and I'm in no rush to leave.

But I'm not going to be able to keep stalling forever, and I'm hoping that I'll get an update any second now about exactly how long I have to do this before I really do have to get out of here. Fortunately, that update arrives a second later when I see the notification flash up on the screen of my mobile phone, and I click on it to read the new message I have just received.

"Train is late leaving London. New arrival time - 18:53."

I check the time now and see that it is 18:02. We're running almost half an hour behind the original sched-ule. That delay isn't great, but it shouldn't change things too much. Everything can still go to plan, providing there are no more hiccups.

With Louise currently out of the room, I have no need to be discreet, so I type back a quick reply.

"Keep me updated."

'Who are you texting?'

I look up from my phone to see Louise standing in the doorway.

Damn, I didn't hear her leaving the bathroom.

'It's just a mate,' I reply as I lock my phone and put it back down on the mattress under the duvet beside me.

'Sure it's not one of your other girlfriends?' Louise asks, and I think she is teasing me judging by the look on her face, but I have to be careful with my answer, nonetheless. I can't have her look at my phone and see the messages because that would spell trouble for the plan and make it way more complicated than it needs to be.

'My only girlfriend is right here in this bedroom with me,' I reply, and Louise smiles.

'That's the right answer.'

I watch her wander away again, and I'm relieved that she is giving me a minute before she tells me to get up for the tenth time. That's because I need to stay at this flat until I receive the next message from that train, the one that will give me much more useful information than simply informing me of an estimated time of arrival.

I sink back into the pillow again as Louise walks back into the room, holding her own mobile phone.

'My mum's just texted me. Her train has been delayed, so she won't be back until seven now.'

Of course, I already knew that, but I act as if it's welcome news, peeling back the duvet and patting my hand on the mattress, inviting Louise to rejoin me in the warm bed.

'Okay, but only ten minutes,' she says, easily persuaded. 'She's delayed, but she's still on her way.'

'We can do a lot in ten minutes,' I reply with a cheeky smile as Louise gets back into bed, excited by the prospect of passing the time in a much more enjoyable way than it might otherwise have to be.

As Louise snuggles in nearer to me, I make sure to keep my phone a good distance away from her in case a new message should come through. It could happen at any moment and the sooner, the better.

'So what do you want to do?' I say as I begin to kiss her neck, but Louise stops me.

'How about you tell me a little more about yourself.'

That wasn't what I had in mind.

'Come on. We can do something more interesting than that.'

I try to initiate another kiss, but Louise pulls away.

'Seriously. You can't just keep coming around here and getting into my bed. Not unless you actually answer some of my questions.'

I sigh and sit up further in the bed. While this isn't ideal, anything that kills the time between now and when I get the text message from the train is fine by me.

'Okay, what do you want to know?'

It's a pretty open question, but considering I haven't actually told Louise that much about myself, it's a valid one. Besides, it doesn't really matter what she asks me.

I'm going to lie to her anyway.

'I don't know. How many girlfriends have you had before me?'

I roll my eyes. 'Really, that's what you want to know?'

'You said I could ask anything.'

'Fair enough. I've never really had a serious girlfriend.'

'No way. I don't believe you. You're lying.'

'No, I'm not. Remember what you told me once. Guys don't mature as quickly as girls do. I was way too immature to have a relationship when I was your age.'

That is partly true. It's definitely taken me a while to mature, and I did spend a lot of time messing around over the last few years although I don't mean just drinking and partying. I mean three years spent in a prison, but I can hardly just drop that into the conversation and expect to get away with it. Therefore, I'll stick to either being vague or just plain lying.

'So what makes you think you are ready for a serious relationship now?' Louise asks me as she snuggles into my chest.

'I guess I've finally met the right girl,' I reply, and I expect such an answer is going to score me some serious brownie points. That is confirmed when Louise leans up and gives me a kiss on the lips.

She's so easy to manipulate, and I almost feel a little sorry for her considering what I am going to do.

Almost.

'What do you want to do with your life? You know, now you're Mr Mature,' Louise asks.

I take a moment to give an answer, not because I am stuck for one, but because I have to make one up. The real answer to that question would be to live abroad, somewhere sunny, preferably Ibiza, where I would enjoy a luxurious lifestyle selling drugs to all the tourists who visit the island to party and blow their cash. But I don't think Louise will be thrilled if I say that, so I'll just play it safe and lie again.

'I wanted to be a doctor when I was younger,' I reply, deciding that is a more socially acceptable choice of profession to have than drug dealer.

'Really? You? A doctor?'

'Hey! What are you getting at? I'm smart enough!'

'Whatever you say.'

Louise laughs as I pull her in close and give her another kiss. Despite everything that is about to happen, I will actually miss her after today. Not enough to cancel the plan, obviously, but enough to look back fondly on these times when I am sitting enjoying a cold drink by myself in twenty-four hours' time. We have had some fun together since we first hooked up a month ago. Back then, I was just out of prison, and all I was looking for was a casual relationship with any woman. That's the thing about spending time inside. You aren't exactly fussy about who you date when you get out. But far from just being a casual fling, this relationship quickly turned out to be so much more. That's because ever since I met Louise and learnt about her life, my dilemma about how I was going to make money on the outside slipped away. It was as if we met by fate rather than the simple swiping of a thumb on a mobile phone app.

'What would your dream job be?' I ask, figuring that making this conversation a two-way thing will keep us lying here for longer.

'I don't know,' Louise replies. 'I like animals, so maybe a vet.'

'Don't you have to be really clever to be a vet?'

'Hey!' Louise hits me playfully across my bare chest, and I grab her hand before she can remove it. Then I pull her in for another kiss, and this time we don't go back to discussing our dream jobs. We're far too busy passing the time in another way.

7

I always feel better once I've lost myself in my writing. All of life's problems seem to fade away into the background, and I'm free to just focus on what I enjoy. That explains why I'm so focused on what I am typing that I fail to notice that the man opposite me is trying to talk to me again. It's only the fact that he waves his hand in front of my face that diverts my attention away from the laptop screen.

'Sorry,' I say as my fingers come to a stop inches from the keys. Once I get started, I don't usually stop until the end of the line. But no such luck today.

'I was just saying that you're going to wear that keyboard out if you're not careful,' he tells me with a warm smile.

'Oh, right. Yeah,' I reply, returning the smile even though my brain is still deep in the story I was just writing.

I'm not really sure that what he just said was worth him interrupting me for, but never mind. I'm just about to get back to work when he speaks again.

'That's the strangest way of playing solitaire that I ever saw.'

I laugh at his witty observation, and my loosening up obviously gives him the confidence to carry on.

'What is it you're writing? If you don't mind me asking.'

I do mind, but I'm too polite to let it show. While I appreciate the attention from the handsome man and even feel a little flattered that he is interested in me enough to try to make conversation, I really would rather just focus on the task at hand. Maybe this guy is looking for something to do to pass the time until his stop, but I don't have that problem. I know exactly what I need to be doing, and it's not engaging in chit-chat.

'It's nothing,' I reply with a shrug, but he doesn't let me get away with it that easily.

'Hmmm. If it's not work, and it's definitely not solitaire, what could it be?'

Even though I'm a little irritated, I smile at the man, mainly because he is still smiling at me. As I look at his brown eyes, his slick black hair and his designer stubble, I feel a slight bubble of excitement inside me that comes from being around somebody attractive. I really should concentrate on my work. But the more he looks at me with those dreamy eyes, the more I'm hoping he keeps on talking.

'I think I know what it is,' he says smugly.

'Oh, yeah?'

'Yep. You're writing a book because you want to be an author and you don't want to have to commute into London anymore.'

I pause because I'm actually impressed, as well as a little shocked. Is he that good at guessing, or am I just that obvious?

'That's right. How do you know that?' I ask him, intrigued to know.

He seems satisfied with himself as he leans forward across the table, closing the gap between us considerably.

'Can I let you in on a little secret?' he says, and with his handsome face this close to mine, he can almost do whatever he likes.

'What's that?'

'I'm sorry to say, but you're not exactly special.' Then he sits back and winks at me.

Oh. That wasn't what I was expecting.

'Excuse me?' I ask, feeling a little deflated.

'I don't mean it like that,' he assures me. 'I'm sure you are very special in your own unique way. I just mean the whole wannabe writer thing you've got going on here. Let's just say you're not the only one on this train who is dreaming of better things.'

I frown because I'm not sure what he means until he points something out behind me and tells me to look.

I turn around and glance down the carriage.

'See that guy there with the iPad?' he asks me. 'He's writing as well.'

My eyes scan the carriage before I notice the bald-headed businessman a couple of rows down typing on the device on his lap.

'How do you know he's writing? He could be doing anything.'

'Trust me, he's writing. I'm guessing it's an action thriller about an undercover spy travelling the world. He looks the type who pretends to be James Bond when he's not selling insurance in a bad suit.'

I laugh.

'And you see that guy a couple of rows further down typing on his phone? The one with the wild hairstyle?

He's writing a science fiction novel. Lots of epic space battles in that one.'

I see the young man with an unruly mop of purple hair staring at his phone and smile because I get what game this stranger is playing. But I'm having fun, so I want to play along too.

'What about her?'' I ask, nodding towards a woman behind him who is also working on a laptop.

'That's an easy one,' he says as he turns and looks in her direction. 'She's trying to make it as an erotic author. Very steamy stuff. I can't be sure, but I believe her pen name is Lola Lipstick.'

'I heard it was Penelope Passion.'

He laughs, seemingly approving of my attempts to join in the game.

'See what I mean?' he says, gesturing to all the people in the carriage around us. 'Everybody here is trying to become a writer. But now we know what their books are about, the only question is, what are you writing?'

I know I shouldn't be allowing myself to be this distracted during what little time I actually have in my day to work on my own thing, but I'm enjoying myself too much to put a stop to this conversation. Instead, I let out a deep sigh and go for it.

'I'm writing a psychological thriller,' I confess.

'Interesting. Let me guess. Your hero is an ordinary woman who ends up in an extraordinary situation.'

'Something like that.'

'How many words have you got?'

I make a check on the count at the bottom of my screen.

'Just over forty thousand so far.'

'Wow, you are a writer!' he says, and even though I know he is joking, it still feels good to hear somebody call me that. He is the only one who has ever done so, besides me, of course.

'I'm trying,' I confess. 'But it's tough. There's so much competition. Lola Lipstick has more fans than I do.'

He laughs again, and I'm actually starting to think this might be going so well between us that it could lead to something beyond just a simple train-journey chat. But then I remind myself of my track record when it comes to the opposite sex, and I'm quickly brought back down to earth with a bump.

There's a reason why I haven't dated anyone in so long.

Every guy has ended up making my life worse than it was before I met him.

'So what happens to this character of yours?' he asks me, and I can't believe he is genuinely interested. 'Does she have to deal with a cheating partner? A murderous villain? A back-stabbing best friend?'

I realise at that moment that while I have been working on this book for many months, I haven't actually told anyone about the story. That's for two reasons. One, I'm a little self-conscious about people thinking it's a load of rubbish, and two, nobody has been curious enough to ask me yet, including my own daughter. Until today. This handsome stranger actually wants to know about me and my writing.

I guess I should just tell him, then.

'It's about a single mum forced to do some things she doesn't want to do for money.'

Well, they do say write about what you know.

'I won't bore you with the details,' I continue, 'but one of those things she ends up doing goes wrong, and she has to fight for her and her daughter's life.'

I'm expecting him to give me some generic words of

encouragement like "well, good luck with that" or "sounds great, I'm sure it'll do well". You know, the usual things people say when they are secretly thinking that nothing is going to come of it. But to my surprise, he actually seems interested in knowing more.

'I'm fascinated by people who seem ordinary but possess such talents in private,' he says to me, and I'm flattered he is referring to me as talented. At least I think he is. He could just mean other people, I suppose.

'I don't know about that,' I reply. 'But I love writing, and they do say that the key to a happy life is to do what you love, so here I am.'

'So why aren't you doing it full time?'

'Well, I'm not getting paid for it yet.'

'No, but you will do one day, right? You have to believe in yourself.'

I smile again, and the longer this conversation goes on, the more it reminds me of how much I have needed one just like this. It would have been nice for Louise to be the one saying these things to me, but she doesn't approve of my goals and thinks I'm wasting my time. Yet here is a complete stranger who seems to think that I have what it takes to make it as an author.

Maybe I was wrong.

Maybe my luck with guys is starting to change.

'Well, actually, I've recently quit my job in London, and my last day is on Friday,' I confess, feeling my heart beginning to race as I do. But I don't feel quite as nervous now as I did when I told my boss that I was leaving. He was shocked to hear me tell him that I was handing in my notice, but he was even more stunned when I told him the reason why.

'Are you sure you know what you're doing?' were his exact words after learning I planned to make a go of it as a writer, and it was hardly the confidence boost that

I needed to assure me that I was doing the right thing. But thankfully, I get a better reaction this time.

'You have? That's amazing!' he cries. 'Well done, you!'

I accept the praise graciously, but my heart is still hammering away inside me. It feels good to talk about myself with somebody else, but it's a little nerve-racking too. I guess I'm afraid of somebody telling me that I'm making a massive mistake and that I'll be broke and living on the streets when my book flops and I can't get another job.

Somebody other than my daughter, of course.

'Thank you. But the hard work starts now,' I say rather sensibly, and I mean it. I have a mountain to climb if I want to escape this train ride for more than just a year or two, and I know there will be some rocky times ahead.

'In that case, I'll let you get back to it,' he replies, and he settles back in his seat and takes out his phone.

I appreciate the fact that he is willing to let me get on with my writing, but now we have spoken this much, I don't want the conversation to end here. It was going so well.

The sensible part of my brain is telling me to start typing again, but the part that is seeking adventure makes me blurt out the next question.

'And what is it you do for work?'

The man looks up from his phone, and I hope he doesn't mind me returning the questions.

'Have a guess. But I'll give you a clue. I'm not an erotic author.'

I laugh. 'Okay, thanks for the heads-up.'

I take a moment to think of my answer. Judging by his appearance, he is clearly an office worker, but his confidence leads me to think that he isn't just some lowly guy at the bottom of the chain. He could be a bit of a high-flier. A lawyer? A banker? A CEO? Then again, he is on the half-five train out of London, so he obviously avoids any overtime as much as I do.

Hmmm, I'm not sure. I'll just have to take a shot.

'I think you're an accountant,' I say, veering towards finance because it seems like a safe bet.

To my surprise, the man's expression lets me know that I am correct.

'Wow, good guess. I'm impressed.'

'My talents extend beyond simply punching a keyboard on a crowded train,' I jest, and when I see him laugh again, I can't help but feel like this is actually leading somewhere positive.

I wonder which station he gets off at. I wonder if he is going all the way to Brighton. That would give us another forty-five minutes to get to know each other even more.

I think I would like that.

'So where's home?' I ask him, my desire to know overpowering the part of me that is trying not to appear too keen.

'I'm all the way at the end of the line,' he replies. 'And you?'

'Same,' I tell him, trying to keep a blank expression to not give away how happy I am that he lives in the same place as me.

A nervy glance at his left hand confirms that there is no wedding ring either.

This could be my lucky day.

'Looks like we're stuck with each other for a little while yet, then,' he says, and I can't hide the smile that spreads across my face after that comment.

'It looks like we are.'

8

STRANGER

The train comes to a halt at its first stop outside London, and I watch as several passengers disembark, stepping out onto the sun-kissed platform and scurrying off to their homes, where the comforts of a warm meal and several hours spent in front of a television set await them. Those with a shorter commute are now free. It's just those hearty souls like Amanda who still have so much more journey time to endure.

The train is still relatively busy but not as bad as it was when we first left London, and I have been waiting for this particular stop before I make my move on the woman opposite me. We've been chatting innocently for most of the journey, and I can tell that Amanda likes me based on both how the conversation has been going and the fact she keeps self-consciously fiddling with her hair and glancing up at me whenever she thinks I'm not looking. She currently has her eyes back on her laptop screen, but I bet she is just dying for me to say something else to her again, so I'd better not disappoint her by keeping her waiting too long. A quick check on my stolen watch also reminds me that I'm not the only one who could be disappointed if I don't reengage her soon.

It's forty minutes to Brighton.

'Tell me about your daughter,' I say just after the doors close, and the train slowly moves along the platform again.

Amanda looks at me as if she might have misheard. 'My daughter?'

I nod my head to telegraph that she heard right, and for the first time since we met, Amanda looks puzzled. It won't be the last time, though.

'How do you know I have a daughter?' she asks me, and I imagine she is starting to worry that the perfect man she has met on her way home might not be so perfect after all. But like most things in life, I have an answer for it.

'Your book. You said the main character is a single mum who ends up fighting for her and her daughter's life. I could be wrong, but I'm guessing that character is loosely based on yourself.'

Amanda instantly looks down at her screen, clearly feeling a little shy about being so transparent.

'It's okay,' I assure her. 'Most writers write what they know. Even Lola over there,' I say, nodding at our fictional erotic writer.

She laughs again and I'm finding it's easy to get that reaction from her.

'Some of it might be based on personal experience,' Amanda confesses. 'But only a little.'

'So tell me about her,' I say again, pressing her for more.

I can see that Amanda is wary of discussing this topic, and I know why. From what I have gathered, things aren't particularly rosy between mother and child. I imagine it's draining to live with a family member you clash with on a daily basis. But Amanda had better get comfortable talking about her daughter because she is the reason I am here right now, and we have much to discuss before we go our separate ways.

'She's seventeen,' Amanda tells me, allowing her hands to rest on the table in front of her keyboard. 'Bright girl but got no direction in her life. She's not like I was at her age.'

'You knew what you wanted to do?' I ask, and Amanda nods.

'I wanted to write.'

I smile at her again, mainly because I want her to feel as if she is chatting to an old friend and not just some random guy she has met on the train home. I bet she wasn't expecting a free therapy session on her journey this evening. But I'm certain that I am getting more out of this than she is. That's because I'm making sure to confirm a few things in my mind before I say what I came here to say. I'm impatient to just get to the point, but rushing in my line of work only leads to one place.

Prison.

'She's only young. She'll figure things out,' I tell her. 'Just like her mother did.'

I wink at Amanda again, and she gives me that pretty little smile of hers. I'll miss that in a few minutes' time.

'What's your daughter doing right now?' I ask, picking up the pace just like the driver of this train is doing as we head further out of the urban area and headlong into the great British countryside.

'She's at home, probably on the sofa, probably not moved all day.'

'By herself?'

Amanda nods.

'That's interesting.'

'What is?'

'The fact that you trust her to tell you the truth about what she is doing.'

Amanda studies me for a moment, but I give nothing away, and the silence between us gradually moves from normal, to awkward, to just plain unsettling.

'I'd better get back to work,' Amanda says, looking back down at her screen.

'But there's so much we haven't talked about yet.'

Amanda looks back up at me a little warily this time. 'Like what?'

'Like how can a single mum quit her only source of income so she can pursue a career with so much risk? Giving up a guaranteed wage for what? Some book she writes on her laptop on her train ride home? That seems like quite the risk to take. Unless…'

I pause for a little dramatic effect between us, allowing Amanda's imagination to run riot while I do.

'Unless what?' she asks when she can't take it anymore.

'Unless you have a considerable amount of money saved away.'

I sit back in my seat and smile at Amanda as she processes my suggestion.

'What are you talking about?' she asks me, studying my face.

'Don't give me that,' I reply with a wide grin. 'You know exactly what I'm talking about.'

9

AMANDA

Why did this have to suddenly get weird?

I was so close to asking this man his name and maybe even enquiring about the possibility of the two of us going for a drink, but now he's starting to give me the creeps. He seems to be suggesting that he knows something about me, though what that is, he hasn't said yet. He just keeps alluding to it. But the fact he has brought up the subject of money, or rather my money, is making me think that it is time to bring this conversation to a swift end before it can get any worse.

'Sorry, I'm not sure what you mean,' I say, and my eyes flit from the man to the carriage behind him. I'm looking to see if there are any other tables free for me to sit at and continue my writing. The vibe at this table has changed dramatically, and I don't wish to be around it any longer. But there are none. Never mind a table seat, there are no unoccupied seats at all, and I don't expect there to be until we have passed through the next stop at least.

Damn you, rush hour.

If I do get up now, then I'll end up standing all the way back to Brighton, and that wouldn't be fun. It would also be unfair because I got this seat, and I shouldn't have to leave it because a fellow passenger is making me feel uncomfortable. That's why I look back to the man sitting opposite me and frown.

Why should I have to move? I'll simply ignore him and go back to my writing.

I look down at my laptop and try to pick up the thread of my story where I last left it, but then the man speaks again.

'Don't be rude. We're talking.'

I look up from the screen against my better judgement and make eye contact with him again, but those eyes don't look so dreamy anymore. Now they appear to be staring straight into my soul.

'Sorry. I really need to concentrate on this,' I try, but I have a feeling that won't be enough.

'And I need you to concentrate on me because what I am about to show you is very important,' he says, and I watch as he takes his mobile phone out of his pocket.

'What is it?' I ask as he scrolls through his phone, even though I'm wary of what the answer could be. But I don't have to wait long to find out. He turns his device around and holds it out towards me, and suddenly it's as if all the noise and colour on this train is sucked out of the carriage.

It's a photo of two people in bed. It looks like a selfie of a happy couple, and I can see smiling faces and bare shoulders, all of which contributes to my confusion and surprise when I recognise the young woman.

It's Louise.

'Where did you get that?' I ask, reaching out for the phone to take a closer look, but the man swipes it away just before I can get it.

'A friend sent it to me an hour ago,' he says, seeming to take some delight in my failed attempt at grabbing his device. 'It seems your daughter has been keeping secrets from you.'

'What are you talking about?'

My voice is raised now, and we attract the glances of a couple of commuters across the aisle. The man opposite me stays quiet until he is sure the passengers have gone back to their own business.

'Stay calm, and Louise will be okay,' he tells me, his voice much lower than mine was. But I'm not feeling calm, especially after he has just used my daughter's name.

'How do you know my daughter?' I ask again, and I notice that my hands are gripping the edge of the table now as I speak.

'Like I said. My friend is with her, and let me tell you, he knows her a lot better than I do, if you know what I mean.'

He gives me another wink, but unlike the ones that preceded it, there's nothing friendly or flirty about this one.

'I don't understand. Who are you?'

'I'm like everybody else here—just a guy on a train putting in an honest day's work.'

'What do you want?'

'Again, I just want what everybody else here wants.'

'Which is?'

'More money, of course.'

I'm doing my best to stay calm, but it's hard. 'Money? What money? What are you talking about?'

The stranger shakes his head with a smile. 'Stop messing about. You know what I mean. Your money.'

I knew it. A handsome man striking up a conversation with me on a train. Showing an interest. Complimenting me. Flirting with me. It was too good to be true. There had to be more to it.

And now I know what it is.

Ever since this train left London, I thought I was only giving this man the pieces of information that I was comfortable sharing. But it turns out he already knows plenty about me, and instead of him extracting facts from me, now it's my turn to try to get them from him.

'What are you talking about?' I ask in response to the money statement.

'Don't play games. I know you have money at your flat. I know it's in the safe in your bedroom. The only thing I don't know is how to access it.'

I'm trying to remain calm, but inside I'm freaking out.

This cannot be happening.

That safe is not supposed to be public knowledge.

How is this possible? There are only two people in the world who know about it. Me and Louise.

Louise.

Oh, God, what has she done?

I'm trying to give nothing away, but he must spot a flicker of emotion on my face as I think about my daughter.

'Yes, that's right,' he says with a smug grin. 'Louise has been a silly girl.'

I look around the carriage to see if anybody else is looking at us. Is this some kind of prank? Where's the hidden camera? Am I going to be on TV? The thought of that is mortifying, but it's a hell of a lot better than the other possibility.

The possibility that this is real and the man opposite me is trying to take everything in my safe.

'What have you done to her?' I ask, feeling the fear gripping me inside as I wait for the answer.

'Nothing yet. And we won't do anything as long as you give us what we want.'

'We?'

'The man in the photo with Louise that I just showed you. We're working together as a team, and we're a very formidable one at that. He's at your flat right now with your daughter.'

I think about the photo he just showed me of Louise and a dark-haired man who looked to be a few years older than her. They seemed to be lying in bed together and were clearly very comfortable around each other considering their apparent state of undress. While it was a shock to see my daughter's image on this man's phone, it was also striking to me to see her with a guy I never even knew existed. Louise has obviously been keeping secrets from me.

And there was me thinking we already had enough problems in our relationship.

'I don't know what kind of prank you're playing, but this isn't funny,' I say, closing my laptop and sliding it into its bag. My writing is obviously done for the day, but real-life events are proving to be far more unpredictable than anything I could have written in my fiction novel.

'This is not a prank, Amanda,' he states firmly, and I freeze.

He knows my name.

I told him a lot of things about myself during the course of this journey, but I didn't tell him that.

I look around again at my fellow passengers and wonder if calling to them for help might get me out of this scary situation.

'Don't even think about it,' he says as if reading my mind, and I return my gaze to his annoyingly smug face.

'Look, I don't know what you think you know about me, but you're wrong. There's no safe, and there's no money. You've got me mixed up with somebody else.' I go to get up out of my seat, and for a second I think I might just be able to leave. That is until the man speaks again.

'I wouldn't do that if I were you. Trust me. You do not want to test me.'

I pause in position by my seat. Do I believe him and sit back down? Or do I grab my things and get as far away down the train as I can from this guy?

'Just sit down and listen to me,' he says. 'It's in your best interests to hear me out.'

I sincerely doubt that, but how else am I going to know what this is all about?

I slump back down into my seat but keep a grip on my laptop bag and coat in case I need to make a dash for it. Trying to think rationally, I console myself with the fact that this is a very public place, so this man can't do anything to harm me here in front of all these witnesses. There is also the fact that we are on a train that is going to pass through several stations before it reaches Brighton, so I will have the opportunity to potentially escape at any one of those stops if I need to.

Whatever this is, it's going to be all right. I just need to stay calm. Maybe it's not as bad as I think it is. So what if he knows about my safe? As he says, he doesn't know how to access it. That's because I'm the only one who does. Even Louise doesn't know the code, and based on what I am learning now, that is a good thing because it sounds like she has been sharing plenty of information with somebody else about my private life.

'I know who you are, and I know how much money you have in that safe. I know those things because your daughter has told her boyfriend all about you and your savings.'

'Her boyfriend?' I reply. *Is it that serious with this guy?*

'Don't feel bad because she didn't tell you. He's a few years older than Louise, so maybe that's why she didn't mention him. But trust me, you're not the only one who has been kept in the dark about things.'

'What do you mean?'

'The man your daughter has been seeing for the last few weeks is not who he says he is. He's actually a convicted criminal, and between you and me, he is very dangerous.'

'Dangerous?' I say, feeling as if everything is starting to spin. 'What the hell have you got my daughter into?'

'She is the one who has got herself into this. She is the reason all of this is happening.'

'What do you mean?'

'Your daughter has told her boyfriend all about you and your dreams. But what was most interesting was the bit where she mentioned that you have £20,000 locked away in the safe in your bedroom.'

I continue to grip the table with my hands, trying my best not to freak out.

This is a bad dream.

Please tell me this is a bad dream.

'He passed on this information to me a couple of weeks ago, and since then, we have come up with a plan to get that money out of your safe. Tonight is the night when we make it happen.'

I can't believe this. I guess I'm not the only one who has been making grand plans. But whereas mine is only slightly unrealistic, this guy's is downright crazy.

'You must be mad if you think I'm going to give you the code to that safe,' I tell him, doing my best to stop my voice from cracking as I speak. I've decided that there's no point in me trying to deny the existence of the money now. He obviously knows too much. But I can still put up a fight, or at least make it sound like I can.

'I think it would be best for Louise if you did as you were told,' he replies condescendingly, but he doesn't understand the situation. I love my daughter, and I will do anything to protect her, but opening that safe may not be the best way of doing that. In fact, I'm confident it will only make things worse for her, and for me.

With his words ringing in my ears, I reach into my bag for my mobile phone in an attempt to call my daughter.

'I wouldn't do that if I were you. My partner is with Louise right now, and he will know immediately if you phone her to warn her about him.'

I hold off on making the call after his warning but keep my phone in my hand just in case. A quick glance outside the window at the row of houses passing us by tells me that we are coming towards the next station. It wouldn't do me much good to try to run now considering I'm stuck on a moving train. But maybe if I can get off this train when it stops, then I could get help, and all of this might be all right. But we're not at the next station yet.

'Who are you?' I ask the man, trying to keep calm and stall for time.

But the reply I get chills me to the bone.

'Me?' he says with a devilish grin. 'I'm your worst nightmare.'

10

It's time to be honest with Amanda so she knows exactly how precarious a position she's in. I told her that I'm an accountant, but she knows now that I was lying. What she doesn't know yet is what I really am.

'I know you've been working hard on your goals,' I say to the woman across the table. 'But so have I. I spent five years in prison deliberating on my own ambitions, and I learnt a lot of things in that time to make sure I never end up in there again.'

Just the thought of those endless nights inside staring up at the ceiling in my cell is enough to make me shiver, so I take a moment to look outside at the brilliant blue sky to remind myself that I am a long way from there now.

'You're a criminal,' Amanda says scornfully.

'No,' I reply, holding up my hand to correct her. 'I was a criminal. But not anymore. Now I'm a businessman.'

'What are you talking about?'

I place my hands together and rest them on the table

between us, aware that appearing calm and in control will be my best way of frightening Amanda into giving me what I want. I must be cool on the outside because I'm feeling nervous on the inside, but I can't let her see that.

'The reason I ended up in prison was because I let my emotions control my actions. I got too invested in the idea of the prize. Money. Success. I wanted it too much. Much like how you are with your writing, I imagine.'

I know she'll hate the fact that I am assuming things about her.

'You don't know anything about me,' she quickly replies. 'You say you do, but you have no idea.'

'Trust me. I know everything I need to know,' I state. 'I know that you will do almost anything to make your dream come true, but there is one thing that you would give it all up for. That thing is your daughter's life.'

'You're crazy.'

'No, I'm not. I'm clever. You are going to give me the code to that safe so my partner can take the money out, or you are never going to see your daughter alive again.'

I wave my mobile phone in front of Amanda again.

'All you have to do is give it to me, and I can send him a message. We'll take the money and be on our way. Nobody has to get hurt. You and your daughter can carry on as you were before.'

I study Amanda carefully to see what her next move will be. I am confident she will give me the code at some point, but I'm expecting she'll put up a fight before she does. I know I would if someone were trying to take everything I owned. And I'm not wrong.

'I don't believe you,' she says. 'You're not a killer.'

'You're right. I'm not,' I reply without missing a beat. 'I'm a con man. It's my partner James who is the killer.'

Amanda's face falls a little, and I press on to hammer home my point.

'I went to prison for fraud. I was young. I was overeager. I made mistakes, but they were harmless. Nobody got hurt. Everyone got their money back in the end. But James was inside for something else. Something much worse than stealing money. And you'd best believe that people got hurt where he was involved.'

I'm hamming it up a little, but I'm not lying. James is a dangerous man. I might be the brains behind this operation, but he is the brawn, and that is what I need to get across to Amanda so she realises how much danger her daughter is in.

'We were cellmates on the inside,' I tell her. 'Spending all day every day cooped up together, it's only natural that we became friendly. I told him what I was in for, and he told me what he had done. James was in for assault with a deadly weapon. He'd got three years. But he'd have got a lot more than that if the neighbours hadn't called the police when they had. He'd be serving a stretch for murder if they hadn't got there in time.'

Amanda is completely still as I speak to her, probably trying to process all of this information whilst trying to figure out if there is any way out of this that doesn't involve her daughter getting hurt and her savings being taken.

But there isn't.

'How did he find Louise?' she asks me.

'It was actually her who found him,' I reply with a chuckle. 'On a dating app. It's the way of the world these days. Of course, like most people who meet on a dating app, it didn't take them long to end up being intimate. James was just looking for a little fun after so long inside, but then Louise told him all about her mum and how she keeps her money in a safe. James passed that information on to me, we hatched a plan, and here we are. All that's left to find out now is how it is going to end. With the code or with your daughter in a body bag?'

Amanda looks through the window at the houses passing us by, but she won't find any answers out there. I click my fingers to get her attention back onto me.

'It's quite simple, really. Your daughter made a mistake, and now you are being punished for it. But don't make this situation any worse for yourself than it has to be. Just give me what I want right now, and nobody has to get hurt.'

Amanda remains silent for a moment, and the only sound around us is the rumbling of the train's wheels on the tracks below.

'How do I know you're telling me the truth?' Amanda eventually asks. 'How do I know Louise is with that man?'

'I just showed you the photo, didn't I?'

'That could have been taken any time.'

I shake my head. 'It was taken today,' I assure her. 'James has been visiting your daughter at your flat while you have been in London working.'

Amanda looks defiant, but she does well to keep her voice calm. 'Even so, that doesn't prove that he is there right now. Let me speak to my daughter. I need to know for sure before I do anything else.'

I shake my head to let her know that I'm the one who makes the demands, not her.

'You're in no position to tell me what you want.'

'And you're in no position to get my money unless you get that code, so I guess we're both screwed,' Amanda fires back, and even though it's annoying, I'm impressed by her spirit.

I check my watch. There is time for a short call, I suppose, and if it helps speed things up, then I guess I'll allow it.

'Say I did let you call your daughter. How will it prove anything? She's hardly going to tell you that she has a guy in the flat with her, is she?'

'I just need to ask her a few questions. I know when she is lying to me, so I'll know if she is actually alone or not.'

I think about it for a second but decide that I don't have much choice. Amanda is a tough cookie. I can see that with how calm and logical she is being in the face of such pressure. But she isn't stupid. She will know that she can't take any risks until she knows her daughter is safe for certain, which is why I am willing to let her take out her mobile phone.

'Okay. You can make the call. But listen to me and listen good. If you make any attempt to try to warn her, then I will call James, and Louise will be dead before you even get a chance to hang up. Don't mention me. Don't mention the money. Don't mention anything out of the ordinary. Two minutes. That's all you get.'

Amanda nods as she looks down at her phone, and I watch her as she presses a few buttons before holding her device to her ear.

Her two minutes start now.

11

I pray that Louise is going to answer the phone and not ignore my call like she sometimes does, although considering our last conversation ended with her hanging up on me, I'm not optimistic. But I need her to answer now. I need to find out if what this man tells me is true.

I need to know if she is in danger.

Keeping the phone pressed to my ear, I listen as I hear two rings go by. Then three. Then four.

Pick up the damn phone, Louise.

'What?'

It's an instant relief to hear my daughter's voice at the other end of the line, even if she is greeting me in her customary way that tells me she doesn't appreciate the interruption.

'Hey, is everything okay?' I ask while under the watchful eyes of the man opposite me.

'It's fine. Why?'

I have to remember not to give anything away, so I try to think of a reason for my sudden concern. 'You didn't text me back when I told you my train was delayed,' I say.

'So?'

'I was just checking you got it.'

'Yep, I got it, so you can relax now. Thanks for that.'

I ignore my daughter's sarcasm and press on with what I really want to know.

Is she alone?

'What are you doing right now?' I ask, averting my eyes from the man and looking out of the window. The train is travelling a little slower now that we are approaching the next station, and the closer we get, the more I feel the urge to run.

'I'm just at home. What do you think I'm doing?'

I really wish my daughter wouldn't treat every single one of my questions like I'm picking a fight, and especially now when I'm trying to determine a potential threat level.

'Whereabouts are you? The kitchen? The bedroom?'

'Why the hell does that matter?'

'I just want to know where you are.'

'I'm in my bedroom. Happy now?'

I'm not happy. Far from it. That's because I still can't tell if my daughter is safe or not.

My tormentor taps his finger against his watch to remind me that I haven't got all day, so I just blurt out the question I need to know the answer to.

'Is there anyone with you in the flat?' I ask, and the man glares at me and reaches across the table to indicate that I'm pushing my luck, but I lean back in my seat and wait for the answer.

'What?' Louise replies.

'I'm asking if you are on your own, or is there anybody with you?'

The line goes quiet for a moment, and I fear the

worst, especially when I see the man take out his mobile phone and hold it up to remind me that he is prepared to make a call of his own.

'Why would you even ask me that?' Louise eventually replies.

'Just answer the question,' I say, my voice cracking a little.

'Yes, I'm on my own!' Louise replies, her voice raised. 'Why are you being so weird?'

My heart sinks at that moment because I know that she is lying to me. She always gets louder and more defensive when she is trying to hide something. She has always been like that, from when she was a child trying to cover up a broken ornament to being a teenager trying to fib her way out of the real reason why she ended up in detention. I know when she is telling the truth because she just mumbles her responses. The fact she is so emotional right now tells me she has something to hide.

'I'm sorry. It's okay,' I say. 'I'll be home soon, all right? I'll see you then. We'll have that takeaway, yeah?'

'Fine,' Louise replies, and then the line goes dead.

I lower my phone, but before I can put it back in my handbag, the man snatches it from my hand.

'Hey!' I cry, but he barely even flinches as he slots my device into his suit pocket.

'How was your chat?'

'Give me my phone back!'

'Not until you give me what I want. So what do you say?'

I can't bring myself to answer him right now because my head is swimming. It's one thing to find out that Louise has been keeping a secret boyfriend from me, but it's another to learn that what she has done has put everything I have ever worked for at risk.

I don't want to believe any of what this man has told me is true, but I'm afraid I'm going to have to. The photo of Louise and James in bed together. The way she spoke to me when I questioned her. And the sheer number of things this man sitting across the table knows about me.

There is no way any of this could be happening if it wasn't true.

'I believe you,' I say.

'Good. Now we've got that out of the way, how about you give me the code, and we can get this over with before we waste any more time?'

The man holds his mobile phone in his hand, and I can see the screen is open on a new text message. I assume he is going to send the code to the safe to James just as soon as I give it to him. Then they will take everything I have and disappear into the night, leaving me with nothing by the time I get to Brighton except a flat I can no longer afford and a daughter who will hate me even more when we have to move out of it.

Why did I quit my job? Why did I put myself in this position?

Why did this have to happen?

But it's not my fault. It's not Louise's either, even though I am mad at her for telling some guy she met on a dating app all about the money I have stashed away. The only person at fault is the man sitting opposite me.

The man with the smug look on his face.

I feel the brakes engaging on the train and look out the window to see the station platform coming into view. I'm almost halfway home now, but this journey has been unlike any I've experienced before. I thought I was done with this commuter route. I thought my life was going to get better after this week. I thought I was finally going to have everything I've ever wanted. But now it's over. I'm going to have to give this man the code to the safe because I can't risk anything bad happening to Louise. I'll be broke, but at least she will be okay.

I guess I'll just have to start again.

I guess this is it.

But then I see the bright green colour of the high-visibility jacket on the platform as the train slowly comes to a stop, and suddenly I have hope. It's a police officer. He's standing right there on the other side of the glass. If I could just get to him and tell him what this man is doing, then he could arrest him and stop him from contacting the man with my daughter. Then the police could go round to my flat and make sure Louise is okay. There might be a way out of this that doesn't involve me having to give up the contents of my safe.

I have to try because I can't afford not to.

I wait for the train to come to a complete stop before I make my move. Jumping up from my seat without stopping to collect my things, I turn and run down the carriage, ducking around a fellow passenger in the aisle as I go.

'Hey!' the man calls after me, but I don't turn back. I'm determined to get off this train and reach that police officer outside.

I squeeze myself past several other passengers who have left their seats and are gathering up their belongings, and push on towards the doors. A quick glance over my shoulder tells me that the man is in pursuit, and he is closing on me.

I reach the end of the aisle and break out into the area by the doors, but they are still closed. They won't open until the driver pushes the button, and they only do that several seconds after the train has come to a complete stop.

'Come on!' I cry as I punch the button on the wall to release the doors. But it's not yet lit up, and I know that it won't work until it is.

I look behind me again and see the man is almost upon me. He's going to grab me. I was an idiot for running.

Why didn't I just stay in my damn seat?

Then I see the light go on behind the button. I can open it now.

I push my fingers against it, and the doors to the train slide open, allowing me to step out onto the platform.

I look for the police officer as soon as I'm off the train, and I see him several yards further along the platform with his back to me. Dozens of passengers are streaming off the train from the other doors, and I almost lose sight of the policeman until I see another flash of bright green. I'm just about to call out to him when I hear the voice behind me.

'Get back on this train, or Louise is dead.'

I turn around and see the man standing in the open doorway with his mobile phone to his ear. 'I'm ringing James right now,' he tells me. 'One word from me and she's gone forever.'

My heart feels like it could explode in my chest as I look back up the platform in the direction of the policeman. He's close enough for me to call him but not close enough to stop the man making the call that could end my daughter's life.

'He might be able to help you, but he won't be able to save Louise,' he says, and I turn back to see him shrugging. 'All I have to do is give the word and she will be dead within a minute.'

Several passengers hurry past me on their way home as I stand on the platform, trying to decide what to do. I thought I had a chance to stop this, but now I see that I don't. He is right. Even if I do make it to the police officer and tell him what is happening, and even if they apprehend this man on the train, they will be too late to stop James at my flat. I might save my money, but I could lose Louise.

Then again, I could lose Louise if I give up the code and they discover what else is in my safe alongside that money.

With everybody here having disembarked, the train is preparing to leave again, and I see the conductor on the platform glance up and down the body of the vehicle before putting the whistle to his lips. As soon as he blows that, the doors will close and the train will leave this station. If that happens, the man will be gone, and I'll be powerless to stop him or his partner harming my daughter then.

'It's now or never, Amanda,' he says from the open doorway, the phone still pressed to his ear.

I take one last look down the platform at the police officer.

Then I get back on the train.

12

I walk behind Amanda as she makes her way back to our table, ignoring the puzzled looks from the passengers who have remained on this train. They are presumably wondering why we just made a mad rush for the exit only to be retaking our seats again, but I don't care what they think. I'm just glad I stopped Amanda before she did anything stupid. While it would have been no trouble for me to call James and tell him to punish Louise for her mother's mistake, I'd much rather we stick to the plan that ends up with me getting my share of the £20,000 in the flat in Brighton.

As we retake our seats and the train pulls away from the platform, we are back on track, literally.

'Do you feel better for getting that out of your system?' I ask Amanda as I check my watch for the time. That little charade only wasted a couple of minutes, but I'm growing impatient now, and I imagine James is too.

'Why are you doing this to me?' Amanda asks, sulking in her seat.

'It's not personal. Just bad luck, I guess.'

'You don't have to do it.'

'I'm afraid we do. You see, we need the money.'

'I need that money!'

'But you need your daughter more.'

Amanda can't really argue with that.

'Look, if it's any consolation, I'm very impressed that you were able to save up such a good sum of cash,' I say. 'And if you can do it once, I'm sure you can do it again.'

'How? I don't have a job after this week!'

'Keep your voice down,' I remind her as a couple of passengers look in our direction again.

I wonder if they think we are having some kind of lovers' tiff. If only they really knew what was happening. It would certainly give them something to talk about in the office tomorrow.

I look back at Amanda to see her staring despondently out of the window, and it is a little difficult not to feel some sympathy for her. But sympathy never got anybody paid.

'Look, let me make this as clear as I can for you,' I say as I lean forward in my seat and rest my arms on the table between us. 'You will give me that code to your safe, or your daughter will die. And we're not messing about. Either you pay or your daughter will. It's as simple as that.'

I sit back in my seat when I've made my point, and I expect that to be the end of it. But Amanda still seems reluctant.

'How did you do all this?'

'All of what?'

'This. How did you know where I'd be? Which train I get? Which table I would sit at?'

I smile because that's easy to answer.

'Like most people, Amanda, you are a creature of habit. As soon as James told me about the money in your flat, I began to follow you. You wouldn't have noticed me, but I have been watching you for several days. I watched you leave your flat in Brighton and catch the 07:40 service into London every weekday morning. I watched you walk to your office. I've watched you take your lunch break. And I've watched you go home again on the 17:35.'

Amanda stares at me in disbelief.

'I followed you everywhere you went. The more I followed you, the more I noticed that you didn't deviate from your routine once. Same trains. Same walk to the office. Even the same pricey salad bar for your lunch, which I was surprised about because I thought you were trying to save money, but I guess you have to allow yourself little luxuries somewhere.'

'I don't believe this.'

'You'd better believe it,' I say, nodding my head. 'The sad thing is that you made this so easy. By being so predictable, you removed all risk for me. Take this table, for example. I've watched you sit here every night on your way home. Not the table behind. Not the table in front. This table. You enter the carriage by the same doors, and you sit in the same seat. So much routine. No wonder you are desperate to escape this life. I'd go crazy too if this were my existence.'

From the look on her face, I'm not sure whether Amanda wants to scream in frustration or burst into tears, but now she knows. That daily grind she hates so much has ended up being one of the things that has led to her downfall.

'And Louise?' she asks me.

'We know she is at home all day, so all my partner needed to do was to call around and get inside this afternoon. Now he's there, I'm here, and we've got everything we need. Everything except that code. So what do you say, Amanda? Are you going to give it to me, or are we going to have to hurt your daughter?'

Amanda doesn't say a word as her eyes burn into me, and I wonder what she is thinking.

'I'm not sure what you have to think about, but don't take too long,' I say as I sit back in my seat. 'You've got until the end of the line to give me that code, Amanda. The end of the line or you never see your daughter again.'

13

I'm on edge now. I have been ever since my mum phoned me out of the blue and asked me if I was on my own. I have no idea why she would have done that unless she knew I was lying to her. But I've been so careful. James only comes around when she is at work, and he has always left long before she returns.

So how could she suspect that I'm not alone?

I try to tell myself that I'm just being paranoid, but it's no good. The chances of her calling me while James is here and asking if I am on my own are too small to be random. She must know about him somehow. But how?

Maybe one of the neighbours in the other flats have seen him coming in during the day and told her. But surely she would have had a go at me there and then. Why ask me the question? Why give me a chance to lie about it if she already knows the truth?

Unless she doesn't know. Maybe she just has a suspicion. Maybe she has no evidence. Maybe I'm not in as much trouble as I think I am. But one thing is for sure.

I need to get James out of this flat now before she gets back.

I leave my phone on the kitchen counter and hurry back into my bedroom, where I'm frustrated to see my boyfriend still lying underneath the duvet. I've been telling him to get up and leave for the last half an hour, but he keeps ignoring me. Okay, I didn't exactly persuade him to leave when I climbed back under the duvet with him earlier, but now I am up again, and I need him to be too. Mum is on her way, and she seems to suspect that I've been lying to her.

'Get up now! I'm not messing about this time!' I say to James as I pull the duvet from the bed and reveal his semi-naked body on the bedsheet.

'Hey! It's freezing!' he cries, but I ignore him.

'Please, James. It's not funny. My mum is coming back!'

I've no idea why he is being like this because he's never done this before. Usually, he is quite keen to leave after he's got what he wanted, but for some reason today he is refusing to put his clothes back on and get out of the flat. It's almost as if he is doing it on purpose to wind me up even more.

'Okay, keep your hair on,' he tells me, but that only gets me even more annoyed.

'I'm being serious! You have no idea how much trouble I'll be in if she finds you here. Get out!'

'Hey, calm down!' James replies, and while he doesn't start putting his clothes back on as I wish, he does at least get out of bed. 'What's wrong?' he asks me, clearly having realised that I'm more tightly wound right now than usual.

I think about not telling him about what my mum said on the phone, but then I figure it's the only way to make him understand why I'm so anxious.

'Mum just called me and asked me if I was on my own.'

'She asked you that?' James replies, looking puzzled.

'Yeah. I don't know why she would do that unless she suspected me of having somebody here, so she must have found out about you.'

'How could she know?'

'I've no idea, but why else would she ask me? You need to get out now. Come on, get dressed!'

I pick up James's jeans from the floor and throw them at him before scooping up his T-shirt and jacket from the other side of the room. I wish he were in as much of a rush to put his clothes on as he was to take them off when he arrived here.

'Okay, okay, I'm going,' he says as he pulls his jeans up and fastens the top button.

'I'm sorry. Maybe you can come around again in a couple of days. I just need to figure out what Mum knows before you do.'

'No problem,' James replies. 'Can I use the bathroom quickly?'

'Be quick!' I tell him, and I push him out of my bedroom as he pulls his T-shirt over his head.

He stumbles into the side of the doorframe as he goes, and I feel bad for rushing him, but not as bad as I would do if my mum walked in and caught sight of a guy coming out of my room.

As I hear the bathroom door close, I check my mobile to see if there are any more calls or messages from Mum for me to worry about. But there are none, which is a mild relief although my paranoia is still in overdrive.

A check on the time tells me that her train is due in thirty minutes, which doesn't leave me long to get James out and tidy up around here, but it should be enough. Maybe I'll do a bit of extra tidying in the kitchen too. That might put Mum in a better mood when she walks through the door, and that might stop her asking me any more questions about what I have been up to all day.

As I wait for James to emerge from the bathroom, I begin the tidying up of my bedroom, throwing the duvet back over the bed and making a quick check on the carpet for any items of clothing that my boyfriend might have left behind. But I think he's got everything besides his trainers, which he left by the front door. There's no T-shirt, trousers, or socks in here belonging to a male that could be discovered and lead to a massive argument. A quick spray of my perfume bottle around the flat should also be enough to mask any masculine scent that she could detect when she walks in. The first time James visited me here, I was so paranoid that I used almost a full bottle of scented spray around the flat after he left, and I know I overdid it because me and Mum could barely breathe for the rest of the night. But at least she couldn't pick up the scent of his aftershave.

Everything looks good.

The only thing that I need to do now is get James out of here.

I wish he'd hurry up in that bathroom.

14

W*here the hell is this code?*
I'm pacing around the bathroom with my mobile phone in my hand, waiting to see the text message come through with the numbers on that I will be able to use to access the safe in this flat. But as of yet, there has been no message since the last one half an hour ago in which my partner told me the new time of arrival for that train. But thirty minutes is a long time. He must have been able to get the code from her by now.

So why hasn't he sent it to me?

Feeling frustrated, I type out a quick message on my phone.

"What is taking so long?"

I hit Send and shake my head. I'd hoped to have been out of this flat already, but I'm still stuck here, and I can't go anywhere until I get that code.

'James! Hurry up!'

I almost jump at the sound of Louise's call from the other side of the bathroom door.

'I'm coming!' I call back, and I decide to flush the

toilet just to make it sound as if I am actually doing something in here.

It's getting increasingly difficult to keep delaying my exit, and while I am prepared to be more forceful with Louise if necessary, it would be much easier if I didn't have to be. But that will only be possible if I get the message I need. With that in mind, I write another text, and this one is more forceful.

"Louise wants me out. Hurry up!"

I press Send and hope that will be enough to get things moving on that train. I'm annoyed at my partner because he hasn't fulfilled his end of the agreement. All he had to do was tell Amanda that her daughter is in trouble and then ask for the code. A mother can hardly say no to that. But the longer it goes without any sign of it, the more I am worrying that something has gone wrong.

The only real risk to this plan not working is if Amanda doesn't give us the information we need. That would be unexpected because, after all, isn't it the job of every parent to protect their child at any cost? I know Louise and her mum don't have the best relationship, but still, it's not that bad that Amanda will sacrifice her daughter to keep her hands on a few quid.

Is it?

The prospect of the money in the safe only a few yards away from where I stand right now is a delicious one, and it's also the reason why I'm growing more impatient by the minute. In my mind, that £20,000 is already mine. It should be in my rucksack now, and I should be long gone from here. But another minute ticks by and there is still no word from that train.

'James!'

Louise calls out to me again, but this time she also tries the handle to the bathroom. Of course, I locked the door behind me just after I entered, but that isn't going to be enough to keep me in here until I get that code, especially if Louise keeps hammering on the door like she is now. I can't have her making too much noise in case it draws the attention of the neighbours in these flats. The last thing I need is them poking their heads out of their doors or, worse, knocking on this front door to see what is going on. I need to keep Louise quiet, but that is easier said than done.

'What are you doing in there?' Louise asks me, and the sound of her raised voice is grating on me more and more.

She is really starting to get on my nerves. I understand that she wants me gone before her mum comes back, but I can't listen to her making that racket any longer, so I rush to the door and unlock it. It flies open immediately, almost hitting me in the face.

'For god's sake. What took so long?' she asks.

'Can't a guy get a little privacy,' I say, shrugging my shoulders and heading back to the bedroom.

'Where are you going? Your trainers are here.'

'I'm just checking I haven't left anything in the bedroom,' I say, stalling as best I can.

But then I feel my phone vibrate, and maybe I won't have to stall any longer. I check the notification on the screen and see it is a message from my partner.

"She made a run for it, but she's back on the train. Code any second now."

Well, that explains the delay. Amanda tried to get away. I guess he has his hands full there just as much as I do here. But both mother and daughter are going to have to be kept in line, and while I can't do anything about Amanda from here, I can certainly do something about her daughter.

"I'm going to have to get physical with her in a

minute," I type back. That threat of violence will hopefully speed things up a little because he can just show my message to Amanda, and she'll see that I'm getting irritated with her stalling tactics.

'Who are you texting?' Louise's voice sounds close, and I turn around to see her standing right behind me.

'No one,' I say, shoving my phone back into my pocket before she can try to grab it.

'Another girl?'

'No, of course not.'

'Show me.'

Louise holds out her hand for me to give her my phone. But I'm not going to do that. Then she'll see the messages about her and her mum, and I really will have no choice but to hurt her then.

'You don't trust me. Is that it?' I ask, shaking my head. I guess I'm going to have to play the frustrated boyfriend part now.

'I did, but now you're being all secretive.'

'I'm not being secretive.'

'Well, show me your phone, then.'

'You show me your phone!' I say, but I regret that when Louise holds out her mobile towards me because that's easy for her to do.

She isn't the one with something to hide.

'This is ridiculous,' I say, stepping away from her and taking a seat on the arm of the sofa.

'I knew it. You're just like all the other guys,' Louise says.

'What other guys?'

'Just show me who you were texting!'

'Why should I?'

I can't believe I'm having to go along with this argument just to kill some time. There was me thinking I got lucky when I met Louise and found out her mum had a small fortune stashed away in her bedroom. But the longer this goes on, the less fortunate I'm feeling.

I want to send another message to chase up that code, but I daren't look at my phone in case it irritates Louise even more. But then she just walks to the front door and opens it, and I guess the argument is over.

'Just go,' she says to me.

I guess this is it. I can't put it off any longer.

'Fine,' I say, throwing up my hands and walking towards the door.

'Don't forget your rucksack,' Louise reminds me, referring to my bag on the sofa.

'I don't need it yet,' I reply, not even glancing in its direction.

'Why?'

'Because I'm not going anywhere.'

Then I turn the lock on the door, which only reinforces my point. 'What are you doing?' Louise asks with a hint of concern in her voice. But I don't care about answering her right now.

I only care about the fact that she can no longer escape.

15

The numbers run through my head over and over again. There's eight of them in total, and in the wrong order, they are useless. But in the correct sequence, they will give the owner access to piles of cash. There's a reason why I'm the only one who knows that sequence, and that was the way it was supposed to stay. You don't give out your credit card number. You don't give out your bank details. And you definitely don't give out the code to your personal safe.

Unless some madman tells you that your daughter's life depends on it.

I've done my best to stall him up until this point. I asked him questions, I called Louise, and I even made a run for it off the train. But here I am again, back in this familiar seat, the same seat that is just one example of how routine my life has become. It's that routine that has allowed this stranger to know my precise habits and thus trap me in this scenario.

He followed me home, and he followed me to the office. He even followed me on my lunch hour. All that time and I didn't suspect a thing. Through the crowd of people who rush around me each day as I go in and out of London, I thought I was the clever one. I thought I was the one with the plan to escape. But it wasn't me, all along.

It was the man following me.

I look at him now, and he is still staring at me. His phone is in his hand, and I know he is just itching to send that code to his partner. But for the time being, that code is locked away in my mind, and it will only come out if I let it.

'Tick-tock,' he says as the train continues to race towards the south coast, but I don't need reminding of how long we have got until we reach the end of the line. I've taken this route so much that I almost recognise every field, tree, and fence on the other side of this window. That's because I didn't always use this time to write. For a long time, I simply sat in my seat and stared out of the window despondently during my commute, dreaming of an escape but unable to make it a reality. Sometimes I would distract myself with a game on my phone, or a song in my headphones like most other passengers do, but most of the time I would just look through this window. Even here, as the train moves through these wide-open green spaces, I always felt restricted and squashed in. It was almost as if the feeling of freedom you got from seeing the rolling hills outside was just an illusion, and life was really nothing more than a series of cages and traps.

This train. That desk. My flat. Everything in my life is keeping me restricted and tied down when really all I wanted was to be out there, in the open space, free to go wherever I want, do what I want, and be who I want. I guess that's why Louise wants to go travelling. She wants exactly the same things as I do.

She just wants to be happy.

Maybe I should have been more understanding with her. Perhaps I should have given her some of my money so she could have left these shores and broadened her horizons. Sure, I'd have had fewer funds for myself if I did that, but at least my daughter wouldn't hate me. But now I'm going to lose my money anyway, and Louise will hate me even more because that money is going to neither one of us. It might be her big mouth that got us into this mess when she told her "boyfriend" about the safe in my bedroom, but I doubt she'll fully accept the blame. Besides, it's my big mouth that let her know about the safe. I should never have told anybody about it. Not even my daughter. But it's hard to keep secrets from someone you live with, especially when they are family.

'I don't mean to spoil your enjoyment of the view, but your daughter is presently sitting at home with a very dangerous man,' he says calmly as my eyes gaze at the picturesque scenery whizzing by outside.

But while the view on the other side of this glass has always remained the same, my mood when looking at it has changed over the years. Whereas before I was often feeling helpless and detached, I operate on much firmer traits like grit and determination these days. I learnt a long time ago that feeling sorry for myself wasn't going to get me anywhere.

The only way to get what I want is to fight for it.

With the knowledge that Louise was okay when I spoke to her earlier, I feel confident enough to test the men trying to steal from me. I have to try something, at least until they really force my hand.

I cannot allow that safe to be opened.

'What is it with men these days? Why can't they make their own money?' I ask. 'Why is it that the women of the world are often the only ones capable of fending for themselves anymore?'

I'm hoping to get a little more of a reaction out of him than a simple shrug.

'I don't see it like that,' he replies calmly, not reacting to my attempts to push his buttons. But I won't give in that easily.

'I do,' I reply. 'Every man I have ever known has been just as weak and desperate as you. The need to beg. The need to steal. The need to take what doesn't belong to them. And you are no different. You put on a suit and try to make yourself look successful and important. But in the end, you're just like all of the other men I have ever known. Pathetic losers who have failed at life and now need to use somebody else's money to keep yourself going. Well, bravo. I applaud your power.'

I put my hands together, clapping sarcastically, and he glances around at the carriage a little nervously, as he has been doing whenever I start to make too much noise. But I don't care. If he is happy to make me feel uncomfortable, then I'm more than happy to do the same thing to him.

'Look, it's not my fault that you've been treated badly before. And it's not my fault that you've got all your money in a safe at your flat instead of in the bank. Why have you done that, by the way?'

'None of your business,' I snap back.

'Well, actually, it is because that money is going to be mine now, so I'm interested to know where it came from and why it's hidden away. It's not drug money, is it? Are you a drug dealer? Is that why you're quitting your job?'

He seems to be amusing himself with his joke, but I'm not laughing. Of course I'm not a drug dealer.

I'm much more than that.

'You want to know why I don't keep my savings in a bank?' I ask, leaning forward in my seat towards him in an attempt to telegraph that I am not as afraid of him as he might think I am. 'It's because I got screwed before. Just like you're trying to screw me now.'

16

TWO YEARS EARLIER

I t's a typically blustery day in Brighton as I make my way along the seafront towards the bank. There is a quicker way to get to where I'm going, which involves cutting through some of the streets set back from the Promenade, but I prefer this way for the view. While the waters of the English Channel can't compete with their illustrious counterparts in more exotic locations around the world, I still love being down here by the sea. That's because being by water has always reminded me of the bigger world out there beyond these shores, and while everything in my daily life might seem small and humdrum right now, it isn't like this everywhere. That is the thought that keeps me going until the day I will eventually figure out how to get to where I really want to be in my life.

I pass several people as I walk, some of them looking like locals clutching shopping bags from the local supermarket, but many of them apparently tourists holding more exciting things like ice creams and buckets and spades. It's not a particularly nice day to visit the beach, especially one made from pebbles instead of sand, but that never seems to stop the intrepid hordes who descend on this town every weekend to take a break from their lives in landlocked communities. According to the local council that likes to report on such things, tourists visit here from all over the UK, from as far as Scotland or as close as London, and I wonder how far some of the people in front of me now have travelled today just to be here by the seaside.

I smile as I spot the young girl in the black cagoule skipping along the Prom with her parents on either side of her. She is pointing at the sea and asking her mum and dad if they can see it too, which of course they can because you can't exactly miss the huge body of water to our left. But I'm mainly smiling because it reminds me of my daughter when she was that age. Louise always loved it down here too, and we spent many a happy afternoon playing on the pebbles and splashing at the shoreline. But those memories are now tinged with sadness because it's been a long time since we came down here together. These days, I only venture down this way to run errands, and I know that Louise only comes here to drink alcohol with her school friends. I'm not happy about it, and neither are the local police, but there's simply too much coastline for them to monitor, especially after dark. And my daughter must think I'm a fool if I haven't noticed the occasional bottle of white wine going missing from my stash under the sink.

Thinking about more innocent times with my daughter makes my heart ache as I watch the young girl clutching her mother's hand as she pulls her in the direction of the beach. That is exactly how Louise and I used to be, but those days are long gone now, swept away and confined to the past almost as easily as that sheet of newspaper that I can see fluttering around down on the pebbles.

In the end, it's a relief to see the family ahead of me leave the Promenade and disappear down one of the ramps that lead to the beach because it means I don't have to look at them and their happiness anymore. But it wasn't just the mother and daughter relationship that has me harking back to past times in my life. It was also the sight of the man accompanying them both. He looked protective. He looked dependable. He looked like a guy who had his life in order.

Basically, he looked like the complete opposite of my current boyfriend.

I've been seeing Johnny for two years now, but things have hardly been a picnic between us. While I had envisioned many sunset strolls along the pier with him in the summer and cosy nights in front of the TV in the winter, it hasn't been anywhere near that perfect. That's because, unlike that man I just watched disappear down onto the beach with his family, my partner couldn't be described as reliable and available.

I do my best to keep my hair from blowing all over my face as another strong gust of wind sweeps along the Prom before deciding to cut my losses and cross the street where the tall buildings should offer me a little more protection from the elements. As I walk over the crossing and reach the other side of the road, I think about the argument I had with Johnny two days ago. I haven't seen him since. But unlike all the other times when he would come crawling back and beg for my forgiveness, so far I haven't heard anything from him. Maybe it's for the best. I'm not sure we had the healthiest relationship anyway. It was far too one-sided. I gave, and he would gratefully take.

Affection. Trust. Money.

Mainly money.

But it wasn't that he was greedy. He was just an addict.

Johnny has been battling a serious gambling problem ever since I met him, and despite my best efforts and his best intentions, it is a habit he has never been able to fully control or defeat. While I have done what I could to help him beat his addiction, giving him a place to stay, lending him money, and even attending meetings with him and fellow addicts, it has never been enough. Johnny has to want to help himself, but despite what he keeps promising me, there doesn't seem to be much evidence of him really wanting to do that. Now I feel that our latest argument might have been our last. I haven't seen or heard from him in forty-eight hours. But I know one thing; I'm not going to be the one who makes an effort this time. If he still wants to fight for what we have, then he is the one who is going to have to do the work to keep us together because I'm done with it. I've got enough on my plate without continuing to take on his problems. Trying to hold down my full-time job in London while bringing up a hell-raising teenager is more than enough for any woman to manage without adding a reckless gambler on top of that.

It's not that I'm unsympathetic to Johnny's problems. I am. It's just that while he continues to waste his life on things that aren't going to improve his situation, I've been focusing on things that will improve mine. Finally, for the first time in a long time, I have financial security. I've been saving hard for the past year, putting away as much of my wages as I can in order to give myself and Louise a better life. I am planning to move us out of our tiny flat by the station, where we get woken up by the sounds of the trains at all hours, and move into somewhere a little bigger in a nicer part of town. I've given up many luxuries over the past twelve months in order to do this, including takeaways, holidays, and shopping trips on the high street, but it has been worth it to finally give myself the cushion of having some money saved away. It's not much. Only five grand. But it's more than I have ever been able to save in my life after raising Louise as a single mum for the last fifteen years.

The only real drain on my finances besides my child, our flat, and my commute into London has been Johnny and the money I would give him whenever he hit rock bottom again. It was never much, sometimes as little as ten or twenty pounds, but even so, it added up, and that was money that could have stayed in my bank account instead of ending up behind the counter of a betting shop somewhere in Brighton. Johnny always promised me he would get himself straight and that we would have a healthier relationship, but he would let me down every time.

But no more. From now on, I'm taking back greater control of my finances.

Like today, for example. I'm on my way into the bank to pay in a cheque that I received from one of my colleagues. I had lent her twenty pounds a few months ago when she was struggling to last until payday, and she has finally paid me back, although in the form of a cheque, which was a little surprising and more than a little annoying. I'm not sure why she couldn't just give me the cash, but she is a lot older than me and of that generation that did most of their transactions with a chequebook. But it was nice of her to finally pay me back, and it will be good to have that twenty pounds in my account in a short while. It's not much, but in my circumstances, every little bit helps.

I turn off the Promenade and see the glass doors of my branch on the next street. Pushing the doors open quickly and stepping inside, it's a relief to be out of the blustery weather for a moment. I catch a quick glance of my reflection in the doors as I pass through, and it's evident that my hairstyle has been no match for the bracing wind on the seafront today. But never mind.

I'm here to cash a cheque, not win a beauty pageant.

I'd ideally like to use the self-service ATMs to the left of the banking hall to process my cheque, but I see there is a long queue of people already waiting to use them, so I take my place in the shorter line for the cashier desks instead. In a way, this is better because it's nice to actually talk to somebody instead of just dealing with an automated machine. This is how it was in the old days before technology crept into our lives.

But I still wish my colleague had transferred me the money instead of handing me a bloody cheque.

As I wait in the queue, I check my phone for messages, not that I'm expecting to have any. Sure enough, there are none. Nothing from Louise. Nothing from Johnny. Nothing from anybody. Forget beauty pageants. I guess I won't be winning any popularity contests either.

It takes several minutes of edging along the carpet in this banking hall, but eventually the customers in front of me get seen to, and now it is my turn to step up to the glass screen and speak to the little old lady behind it.

'Good morning. Just paying in a cheque, please,' I say as I slide the piece of paper through the slot onto the cashier's desk.

'You don't see many of these anymore,' she says to

me, waving the cheque at me on the other side of the screen, and I laugh because she is right.

I wish she would tell that to the woman who gave it to me.

I wait patiently as the friendly cashier punches several numbers into her keyboard and glances at her computer screen a couple of times before finally telling me that it is done.

'Would you like a receipt and statement of balance?' she asks, and I tell her that I would.

As she prints one off, I think about how pleasant this woman is. I'm not sure I would be this chirpy if I did her job, but not everybody is like me, I suppose.

Not everybody is forever dreaming of something better just beyond their reach.

'There you go. That's all done for you,' the cashier says as she slides a couple of slips of paper back through the slot, and I take them.

'Thank you,' I say as I turn to walk away, glancing down at the paper as I do.

The first one is the receipt confirming the amount of £20 has been paid into my account today, while the second one is the current balance of that particular account.

It's that second one that causes me to panic.

'Wait,' I say, turning back to the desk and cutting in front of the old man who was just about to take my place. 'This isn't right.'

'What isn't right, dear?' the cashier asks me, my distressed state still not enough to put a chink in her friendly customer service.

'My account. It says that there's only sixty-seven pounds in it. But there should be more than that. A lot more!'

The cashier frowns a little but returns to her keyboard, where she hits several more numbers before reaching out for the edge of her computer monitor and turning it around so that I can see what is displayed on the screen.

'This is your account, correct?' she asks me, referring to the long line of numbers across the top and the sort code beside it.

My eyes scan the numbers, and I can see that they are the ones that belong to me. But before I can answer her, I again notice the numbers at the bottom of the screen, and they are the ones that cause me to grip the marble counter between us tightly.

It's the balance of the account.

Where has my £5,000 gone?

17

AMANDA

I 've just finished telling the man who is trying to take all my money in the present about the man who took all my money in the past.

After that frantic moment in the banking hall of my local branch two years ago, I started to find out why I hadn't heard from my boyfriend in two days. Johnny had cleaned out my account after getting my bank details from the numerous statements I had lying around at my flat, transferring the funds from my account to his. He had got all my money through a combination of my carelessness with my documents and his desperate determination to keep funding his addiction.

He cleaned me out, and now the guy sitting opposite me wants to do the same.

Why does this keep happening to me?

'Even though I told them it was stolen, they said it was my fault for not taking care of my personal details,' I say, hoping that my tale of woe might be enough to give the man opposite me second thoughts about his own plan. 'If a stranger had stolen my credit card from my purse, then they could have helped me, but because it was a boyfriend and he obtained the information easily in my own home, they said I was to blame.'

'I've always hated bankers,' he replies. 'Greedy bastards.'

The irony of what he has just said is not lost on me, and I let him know it with my glare.

'So you never saw Johnny again?' he asks me, and I shake my head.

'I have no idea what happened to him. But I bet he pissed my money away in some bookie's somewhere along the way.'

'Well, thank you for the cautionary tale,' he says, shrugging his broad shoulders. 'But that doesn't do you much good right now. I still want that code.'

I guess sympathy and pity aren't emotions that he gives much time to.

'You're no better than him, you know,' I say, shaking my head. 'He was a thief, and so are you. You should be ashamed of yourself. I worked hard for that money. Why can't you do the same?'

'You don't think this is hard work? You think I want to be here sitting on this train listening to your sob story? I want to be miles away from this place, sitting in the sun with a cold drink in my hand, looking out at the ocean while pretty ladies walk by. Yet here I am stuck with you.'

'That's what you're going to do with my money, is it? Sit in the sun and drink beer. How admirable. At least I have a proper dream.'

He scoffs. 'You think you would spend it more wisely? You'd just waste it while you were trying to get your book published. No joy would ever come from it, and you'd just end up back where you started in a year's time. The only difference is at least I would have some fun along the way.'

'It's my business what I do with it. It's my money!'

The volume of my voice is raised again, but nobody bothers looking over at us this time. Nearly everybody has their headphones in, and their faces are buried in their personal devices. Either they can't hear us, or they are ignoring us. I don't blame them either way. I always hated noisy passengers too.

'You're all the same, you people,' he says, flattening out his tie against his chest. 'Working hard day after day, saving up, and for what? Retirement? Something better down the line? You never stop and actually enjoy yourselves in the here and now.'

'That's how the world works,' I fire straight back. 'It's not all just short-term success. Some things take longer to achieve, and you have to work for them. You can't just take them from other people.'

'That's where you're wrong. I can just take them, and I will. You see, while you and the rest of the people on this train have been busy working hard in your offices, I've been watching you all, and you know what I see? Hesitation. Desperation. Fear. I pity you, and I pity everybody else you work with. You're lacking in confidence to do what you really want.'

'No. I'm not.'

'How old are you?'

I'm surprised by the question. 'What's that got to do with anything?'

'It has everything to do with it,' he says. 'Thirty-five? Forty? Whatever. Why has it taken you this long to go after what you really want in life?'

'Because life isn't that simple!'

'Yes, it is. If you want something, you go and you get it. If you wanted to be a writer, you should have done it twenty years ago. Don't give me excuses, I've been in prison, and I've heard them all before. If only it wasn't for bad luck. If only this. If only that. But now it's too late, and you are being punished for your hesitancy. You're being punished by somebody younger than you who knows exactly what he wants and how to get it.'

After hearing his little speech, I feel like reaching across the table and wrapping my hands around this man's throat, but I resist and not just because I know he would easily be able to fend me off. I resist because there is some truth in what he is saying. It should never have taken me this long to go after what I wanted to do. Yes, life has thrown some curveballs at me, like my unexpected pregnancy and my thief of an ex-boyfriend, but I also know that there was something else holding me back too, and it was something completely in my control.

My own self-belief.

But now that I'm older and wiser, I have that belief. I know what I am capable of, and I know how strong I am in any situation. Yet here is life again, throwing me another curveball. If it were just up to me, then I would fight my way out of this situation and not give in. But it's not about me now. It's about Louise too. I have to do what's best for her, and my tormentor is only too happy to remind me of that as he looks down at his phone and smiles.

'Your daughter is becoming a problem,' he tells me. 'My partner is growing impatient with her.'

'What has he done?' I ask, the fear rising in my throat.

'Nothing yet. But he will do unless you give us that code.'

'I want to speak to Louise again,' I say, holding out

my hand towards him to take his phone. 'I want to know she is all right.'

But he simply laughs and turns his device around so I can see the photo on the screen.

'I'm afraid Louise is a little tied up right now,' he says, and my eyes widen in horror as I see the image of my daughter on the bed with her hands fastened to the bedpost behind her.

18

I've promised James I'm not going to scream again, and in turn, he has promised not to gag me again. But I haven't been able to convince him to untie me from the bedpost, so I'm stuck here as I watch him pacing around the room in front of me while he checks his mobile phone.

I honestly didn't know what was going to happen when he locked the front door and dragged me towards the bedroom with his hand over my mouth, but I feared the worst when he told me that my mum would die unless I stopped trying to get away from him.

With that ominous warning rattling around in my head, I resisted only slightly as James tied me to my mum's bed with the cable tie that he took out of his rucksack and wrapped around my wrists.

And there was me believing that he just kept his gym clothes in that bag.

Now I'm stuck here at the mercy of a man I thought I not only loved but could trust, and I'm terrified. What is he going to do to me? What is he going to do to Mum?

Why is this happening to us?

'James, talk to me, please,' I say after another unnerving moment of silence has passed.

I have asked him several times to explain his plan to me, but the threat of him gagging me made me give it a rest for a moment. I don't want him to stop me speaking because then I really will be powerless to do anything. As long as I have my voice, then I have an opportunity to talk him out of whatever he thinks he is going to do, and I believe that is my only chance.

I could try screaming again, but it didn't do me much good last time. Nobody is at home in the neighbouring flats during the day, so there is no one to hear my cries for help. I know that because I'm home all day, and I barely hear a sound inside this building other than the ones I make. Everybody's at work, and I used to like that I was the only one who wasn't. But now I'm wishing that I had had somewhere else to be today because then I wouldn't have been home when James came around and surprised me.

'Why are you doing this to me?' I ask him, battling back tears. 'I thought you loved me.'

I'm laying it on a little thick, but I did genuinely think we had something special together. I was obviously wrong. Maybe the guys my age aren't so bad after all. I doubt any of them would have tied me to the bed like this.

But James continues to ignore me and still seems preoccupied with his mobile phone.

'Who are you waiting for?' I ask him. 'Why do you keep looking at your phone?'

'Just shut up,' he replies coldly.

'Not until you tell me what this is about,' I fire back. 'Is it my mum? Has she done something?'

James finally looks up from his phone. 'She hasn't done anything. But you have.'

'What are you talking about?'

'This,' James replies, and he turns and opens the wardrobe behind him. Then he kicks the door to the safe that sits at the bottom of the storage unit, and I feel a wave of nausea because I know what he is after now. The safe is buried beneath a pile of clothes that Mum thinks will stop anybody from finding it should they break in. But James has clearly found it, and I know why, but he is more than happy to remind me.

'You told me about this safe, remember,' James says. 'That's why you're now tied up on that bed, and I'm about to open it and take all your money.'

A wave of dread washes over me as he finally tells me what this is all about. Yes, I told him about my mum's safe a few weeks ago, but so what? He knows I can't get into it.

Then I figure it out. I can't open it. But my mum can.

'What have you done to her?' I ask, terrified to hear the answer.

'We haven't done anything yet,' James replies. 'And we won't, as long as she gives us the code to open this.'

He kicks the door again, and I can see that he is getting more frustrated by the second. That must mean that the plan isn't going as well as he had hoped so far.

'Why would she give you the code?'

James suddenly turns back to me with a venomous look. 'To save you,' he snarls. 'Or at least you'd better hope she does.'

This can't be happening. James is using me to blackmail my mum into opening her safe, the safe he only found out about because I blabbed about it to him.

I feel awful for being so careless with what should have been private information.

Mum is never going to forgive me for this one.

'Where is she? Who is with her? Have you got her

tied up somewhere too?' I ask, afraid not just for my own safety now but for hers as well. She isn't as strong as me. She must be so afraid. *And I'm the one to blame.*

'Calm down. Your mum is fine,' James tells me. 'She's on the train, and she will be back in Brighton soon, just like she told you she would be. But she has to give us the code before she gets home, or you won't be here when she arrives.'

'Who is us? Who are you talking about?'

'My partner,' James replies with a sly smile, and the sight of it makes me feel sick. I can't believe this is the man I let into my bed.

'Is this all I was to you? Just a way to make some money?'

'No, of course not,' James replies. 'At first, you were just a way for me to blow off some steam after I got out of prison. I wasn't planning on seeing you again after we slept together the first time. But then you told me about the safe, and that's when I realised that you weren't just some stupid teenager. You could actually be valuable to me.'

There are a lot of things James just said that concern me, but one word jumped out the most. 'You've been in prison?'

James finally stops looking at his phone and steps closer to the bed until he is standing right beside me, glaring down at me as I wriggle on the mattress and try to get free of my restraints.

'That's right. I was only in for assault, but I was around all sorts of people on the inside who had committed worse crimes than me, including murder,' James says. 'And let me tell you something. Once I got to know them, I saw that there wasn't much difference between me and them. There wasn't much difference at all.'

ONE YEAR EARLIER

'Didn't your mother tell you it was dangerous to talk to strangers?'

As greetings go, it was an unfriendly one, but then I hadn't really expected anything less in a place full of criminals, con men and cowards. The words from my cellmate when I met him for the first time didn't put me off getting to know him, but I still remember them to this day, over two years on. Fortunately, we're much closer now, which makes sharing a twelve-by-eight-foot room a little less awkward than it was when I first walked in here. I've since learnt my cellmate's real name, but ever since his ominous greeting, I nicknamed him "Stranger", and he doesn't seem to mind. He wouldn't be sitting across this table from me now playing poker if he did.

Reminding myself of something Stranger taught me, which is to stay present in the moment, I stop reminiscing on how we met and instead focus on the task at hand, shuffling the cards so we can play again.

I love this deck of cards. It's the only thing I have in here that reminds me of my hometown. The back of each card features a photo taken somewhere around Brighton. The Pier. The beach. The high street. The train station. None of the photos are particularly exciting, and they certainly aren't as explicit as the photos on the back of my fellow prisoner's packs of cards, but they are a reminder of where I come from. I don't miss Brighton particularly, but I do miss being free, and these cards are a reminder that there is a world outside these four walls.

'Are you going to deal or what?'

I look up at Stranger staring at me impatiently for the next game to begin, and because this isn't the kind of place where you want to irritate someone, I shrug and deal the cards quickly. Two each. Five face down in the middle. We don't have anything to play for but pride and the tiny amounts of money we earn doing menial tasks every day inside here. So far, I've already lost the £1.70 I made working in the laundry room last week.

While I've always been used to dealing with pathetic amounts of money in the outside world, the man I'm playing with has not. Stranger has been my cellmate for the past two years, but before that he tells me he was quite the high roller in London. He was a grifter, targeting vulnerable marks and tricking them out of large sums of money, which is what landed him in here alongside me, but not before he had a great time flashing the cash in the capital. But just like me, he got caught, so now it's all gone, and he's just as broke as I am.

As I turn over the first three cards in the middle and we begin to play our hands, I study the man sitting opposite me. But it's not from a poker perspective. It's from a personal one. I'm only twenty-one, and my cell-mate is nine years older than me, and that extra experience he possesses has taught me a lot since we have been in here together. I ended up behind bars because of a crime I committed with my fists, but my cellmate is here because of a crime he committed with his brain. That is something I am very interested in because I want things to be different when I get released back into the outside world.

I don't want to go around beating people up for insignificant sums of money.

I want to be smarter, and I want to get some serious cash.

We've already agreed that we will keep in touch once we are both out of prison. We are both due to be released within the next twelve months, and we have decided to work together when that time comes. We might make an unlikely pair with our age gap and varied experiences, but we are different enough to complement each other, and we share the two same burning desires.

We want to get rich, and we don't want to end up back inside here again.

As I turn over the fourth card in the middle and see my hopes of winning this hand shrink, I wonder what kind of schemes we will be able to run together when we are free men. I plan to spend a little time in Brighton when I first get released, seeing old friends and hopefully hooking up with a few old girlfriends before I join Stranger in London, where we will run cons together. At first, my prospective partner told me that I lacked the patience to be a grifter and that the key to successfully taking the money from any mark was to take your time. I agreed that was a skill I wasn't particularly strong on, but I have worked hard on that during my time behind bars. There aren't many places better to help you learn patience than prison.

I was relieved when he told me that he was willing to work with me, and I am sure we can make some good money together, just as soon as we can get away from these poker hands for pathetic prizes and play in the real world for much bigger stakes. We'll both still be young men after we have served our sentences, and there will be plenty of time to earn the kinds of fortunes that I know both of us dream about when the lights go out in this prison, and we're alone on our beds with nothing but our imagination.

As I turn over the fifth and final card and my hopes of winning this hand dwindle even further, I can hear the noise from outside our cell door where the rest of the inmates on this wing are gathered in the communal area, playing table tennis, watching TV, or sitting around chatting. *Murderers. Thieves. Common thugs.* All bundled into one place and expected to exist together without any problems. But while I have witnessed plenty of trouble since I have been in here during my stretch, including threats, fights, and even a riot, I have kept myself out of all of them. That isn't because I lack the necessary tools to thrive in a dangerous place like this. It's because the only problems I want to cause now are in the outside world with my new partner and the sooner I get out of here, the sooner I can start doing some damage where it really counts.

As my cellmate turns over his cards and shows that he has beaten me again, I smile, not because I'm happy to lose, but because I know we are both going to win in the long term. As soon as we get out of here, there is nothing that is going to stop us. I want to succeed badly. And I know that he does too.

'Nice hand,' I tell him as he collects the cards and

prepares to take his turn to shuffle them, but he doesn't offer anything back. Not that I expected him to. Knowing him as well as I do now, his mind will already be on the next hand because that's how he likes to think. He's always planning several steps ahead. I guess that's the biggest lesson he has taught me in here.

Make a plan. Execute it. But always have another one to implement immediately afterwards. I will bear that in mind when we get out of here. I will also bear in mind his other piece of advice, the one he reminded me of on the day we met.

'Didn't your mother tell you it was dangerous to talk to strangers?'

20

I want this damn code, and the longer I go without getting it, the more I am prepared to do things that are expected of a man who has spent considerable time behind bars. I'd hate for people to think that I'm not dangerous just because I wear a sharp suit and talk fast. I can be just as dangerous as all those men I met on the inside, the ones with the shaven heads, scarred faces, and murderous eyes. The only reason I haven't demonstrated this yet is because I'm exercising patience. But it's starting to wear thin the longer I go without this code. I can't understand why Amanda is still refusing to give it to me, and the only possible explanation I can think of is that she doesn't fully understand the severity of the situation she finds herself in. Maybe that's my fault.

Maybe I haven't been clear enough.

'Do you enjoy playing games with Louise's life?' I ask the woman opposite me after I have showed her the photo of her daughter tied to the bed.

I had told James before today that he was to do whatever it takes to keep Louise occupied until I was able to send him the code, and it looks like he has done just that. I honestly thought I would have had the code by now, and I know James did too, but things don't always go to plan. A younger man such as my partner might panic in this situation and do something hasty. But an experienced man knows to stay calm and that everything will work out well in the end just as long as you stick to the plan. So that's what I am trying to do right now. I am staying calm, and not even the quick check on my watch makes me concerned. We are twenty-five minutes away from Brighton, and every second that goes by is a second closer to Amanda not giving us what we want, which would force us to hurt her daughter as punishment. But it won't come to that. Amanda might be a little feisty, and she still might be doing everything she can to delay her fate, but it is inevitable, just like mine was on that day I stood in the dock and prepared for the judge to send me down.

Amanda will give me this code. She has no choice if she wants to see her daughter again.

'Seeing as you clearly don't realise exactly how much trouble Louise is in,' I say as I place my mobile phone on the table and rest my hands in my lap, 'let me tell you something about the man your daughter is with right now.'

I notice Amanda's hands are much less relaxed than mine, still gripping the edge of the table tightly, and that sight comforts me. She is angry. She is afraid. I continue.

'James and I shared a cell together in prison, and we became quite close. That's why we decided we would work together on the outside. We complement each other, you see. I provide the brains, and he provides the brawn. I came up with this whole plan when he told me he knew of a safe full of money at a flat in Brighton. In turn, he will be the one who hurts your daughter should you not give us access to that safe.'

Then I sit forward to really emphasise my next point.

'Trust me. You do not want him to do that. I saw what he was capable of in that prison. I saw him fight for his life on more than one occasion, and I saw him come out on top every time. He's a strong man, and he isn't afraid to get blood on his hands. So if I were you, I would give your daughter the gift of life and let me call him off right now, before it's too late.'

I've been exaggerating in my little speech, but that's only because I'm trying to frighten Amanda. I never saw James fight for his life in prison. Generally, the two of us were able to avoid most of the trouble that broke out on our wing during our stretch because we kept ourselves to ourselves and spent most of our time playing poker in our cell. The truth is that you don't survive in prison by fighting; you survive by going unnoticed. Unfortunately, that doesn't make for a very intimidating story, so I've allowed myself to be a little creative. But that doesn't mean James doesn't possess the ability to carry out violence. Far from it. It's just that I have gotten him to a place where he won't do it until I tell him to.

'You two must be so proud of yourselves. Threatening violence against a woman. I bet it makes you feel like real men, doesn't it?'

Amanda's response shows she is still not in the mood to give me what I want, and I wonder if I am going to have to call James and get him to actually start hurting Louise after all. It wouldn't be anything big to start with. Maybe just break a finger or two. We could move on to the bigger bones if necessary.

'Twenty-four minutes,' I say after checking my watch again.

I decide that silence might be a little more unnerving

between us for the next few minutes instead of simple threats, so I allow the time to pass by looking out of the window and letting Amanda stew. But then my eyes are drawn back to the table by the arrival of a notification on my mobile phone screen.

It's another message from James.

"What the hell is taking you so long? How hard can it be?"

I shake my head because he's clearly struggling to exercise as much patience as I am. This was what I was worried about. He's nine years younger than me but still likes to make out like he is as good at this as I am. But he'll see how good I am soon enough. He'll see it when I take all the money in that safe for myself and leave him just as defeated as Amanda and Louise.

Just like in the poker games we played inside, I'm thinking several steps ahead and plan to screw James before he has the chance to screw me somewhere down the line. But I can't do that until he has the money in his possession.

"It's coming."

I press Send on my optimistic reply and sit back in my seat. I notice that Amanda has been watching me every time I have used my phone—no doubt worrying about what might be happening—so I might as well tell her.

'I've just told James to be on standby to hurt your daughter. He's more than willing to do it,' I say with a shrug.

Then I place my phone back on the table and fold my arms.

I stare at Amanda until she gets self-conscious and looks away. I like that I have this control over her, but I don't like the fact that I don't know what she is thinking. I don't like it because I know that a person can come up with all sorts of schemes when they are given the time to think.

If this carriage were quieter, then I could be more forceful with her and get the code much quicker, but I'm still betting she will give it up any minute now. I have all the power here while she is the one with everything to lose.

It just remains to be seen what she will lose.

Her money.

Or her child.

21

I'm racking my brains for any way out of this situation that doesn't end in my daughter getting hurt and my safe being emptied. So far, I'm struggling, but I have got one idea, and it might be my only shot.

My tormentor's mobile phone is currently sitting on the table in front of him, and his arms are folded. Maybe if I could grab it and get away down the carriage, I could use the phone to text James and tell him that the plan is off. If James believes it, he might leave my flat, and Louise will be safe. Then all I will have to do is get away from this man on the train. I almost managed it earlier, so I believe I could do it again.

I do my best to appear casual as I sit forward in my seat a little, closing the gap slightly between me and the phone. I'm tempted to just go for it now, but then he shifts in his seat and uncrosses his arms before his left hand comes to rest on top of the phone.

Damn.

'Twenty-three minutes,' he says.

I make sure to not let my eyes linger on the phone in

case he puts it away in his pocket again. I'll just have to stay ready for when he removes his hand. But until then, I need to figure out a way to keep him distracted enough so that he doesn't text his partner and tell him to start hurting Louise.

'The closer we get to Brighton, the more nervous you are going to make my partner, so just do the sensible thing and tell me the code and this will all be over with,' he tries again. 'What do you say?'

I take a moment to think about it, or at least pretend like I'm thinking about it. Of course I'm worried about Louise, but they haven't harmed her yet. That means I still have time. They haven't completely forced my hand, so there's no need for me to show it yet.

There's no need for me to expose myself to the risk of opening that safe for them.

'You think you know everything about me, don't you?' I say, shaking my head. 'You think you're so slick and so clever. But you don't have the slightest idea who I am and what I am capable of.'

'Oh, really?'

'Not the slightest idea.'

'Do you have an example, or are you just trying to chew the fat?'

I pause for a moment. I have to be careful what I do reveal, but I also know I need to keep stalling until he removes his hand from that phone again and I get my chance to steal it.

'How do you think I saved up so much money?'

'That's easy. You have a job.'

I laugh. 'You really think it pays me well enough to save £20,000? Ha. I wish.'

He looks a little perturbed for a moment, and I like that.

'Try again,' I say.

'You inherited it?'

'Nope.'

'I don't know. Maybe you got a paper round.'

I roll my eyes, and that causes him to give up.

'Okay, I have no idea.'

'Exactly. You have no idea. So what makes you think that you can threaten me and my family? You think following me for a couple of weeks shows you who I really am?'

I can tell that he isn't enjoying this topic of conversation quite so much as the one where he got to enforce his power over me, and he sits forward again in his seat, which he only does when he is trying to wrestle that power back.

'May I remind you that you are the mark here? You're the one getting screwed, so what does it matter if there's some things we don't know about you? We know the only things that matter, and that is that you have £20,000 in your safe and a daughter who desperately needs you to give up that money to save her life.'

Refusing to back down, I sit forward myself now, and our faces are only inches apart across the table. Half an hour ago, I would have thought being this close to the man would have meant we were about to kiss. But now I'm doing it to show him that I'm not afraid of him.

'I've dealt with much scarier men than you in my time, and here I am still standing. But good luck with your little plan,' I say, and now it's my turn to give him a wink.

The man studies my face for any sign of weakness, but I show none. I am nowhere near as calm on the inside, but externally I am making sure to give off nothing but strength and confidence. It's a confidence that I hope will continue to make this man doubt the success of his plan if he goes ahead.

After a tense beat, he sits back in his seat, and I glance down at his phone, but his hand is still resting on top of it.

'Twenty-one minutes,' he says, checking his watch again.

He's staying cool and collected, and that's what I must do too. I know time is running out, but that's nothing compared to the time I put into amassing that fortune in my safe.

I know I'm going to have to work hard to keep it in there, but so be it.

I sure as hell worked hard enough to get it in there in the first place.

22

SIX MONTHS EARLIER

I walk into the wine bar right on time. Not early because that wouldn't help my nerves, and not fashionably late because that would be rude. On time. But I'm not the only one. Greg, my date, is entering the bar at the same moment from an adjacent door, and it doesn't take much for us to spot each other across the sea of candlelit tables.

He offers me a nervous wave, and I reply in kind.

This is awkward. This is uncomfortable.

This is exactly how I expected it to be.

After a brief greeting in which he gives me a small kiss on my cheek, we smile at the pretty waitress as she shows us to our table. We follow the uniformed woman past the other candlelit tables, all of which are already occupied with couples enjoying each other's company.

Our table is the one in the corner, and Greg is a true gentleman, making sure to pull out my seat for me before taking his own. Now we are sitting, and the waitress leaves us alone for a few minutes to make our choice from the menu, and there is nothing else we can do to put this off any longer.

It's time to talk.

'I'm sorry. I'm a little nervous,' Greg confesses to me after an awkward moment where the only sounds at our table came from me fiddling with one of the empty wine glasses.

'Me too,' I admit, and we share a nervous laugh.

'It's not my first time,' he quickly adds, and I wish I could say the same.

We both keep ourselves preoccupied by burying our heads in our respective menus until the waitress returns to take our order.

'Are you happy with the Merlot?' Greg asks me, and I confirm that I am because this is his date, not mine.

As the waitress rushes away to fetch us the bottle, I smile at him and decide to get the conversation going, if only to reduce the awkwardness between us right now.

'So, what do you do for work?'

'I'm an architect.'

'Oh, wow,' I reply, genuinely impressed. 'That must be fun.'

'Not really. I have my own business. It's good money, but it's long hours. It doesn't leave me much time for a social life.'

'I see. Would you think about changing careers?'

'I'd love to, but it's tough. You know, going outside your comfort zone and everything.'

Tell me about it.

'But you shouldn't let that put you off,' I say. 'If you have something else you'd rather do, then you should do it.'

He smiles at me when I finish speaking, which at least makes me feel reassured that I'm doing a good job.

'What is it you do?' he asks me, seemingly relaxing a little. 'Besides this, obviously.'

I laugh self-consciously, but it catches in my throat and ends up coming out more like a dry noise. I desperately need some lubrication.

Where is that wine?

'I work in an office,' I say, keeping my answer purposefully vague because that's what I've been told to do by the people who hired me.

'I see,' Greg replies. 'Do you like it?'

'Office work? Yeah, it's all right, I suppose.'

Another awkward silence descends on the table, and I notice Greg shift in his seat a little. I feel bad for him and do my best to think of something to say, but my mind has gone blank. This was a bad idea. I can't believe I thought I could pull this off. This poor guy is paying me good money to be here, and I can't even hold a conversation with him.

Fortunately, the waitress arrives a few seconds later and breaks the ice a little, pouring us each a glass of red wine before leaving what's left in the bottle to sit between us as a reminder that there is more alcohol on standby if needed.

It definitely will be.

'Do you have any children?' Greg asks me rather randomly, and I take a moment to finish my sip of wine before answering him.

'No,' I reply with a shake of the head. 'No children.'

Being vague about my profession is one thing, but I most certainly am not going to tell him about my daughter.

'You?'

'I have two girls. Ten and eight. With my ex-wife.'

I nod my head, remembering that he mentioned his ex-wife in his profile, or rather, he mentioned the fact that he was divorced. I wondered at the time why his marriage had broken up, and I'm still wondering now as I sit here across from him. Did he cheat? Did she? Did they just get sick of the sight of each other like some couples do? Or maybe it's just as simple as him having worked crazy hours in his business and neglecting her. Who knows? It's hardly a question I can ask. But it's a shame for him, whatever happened. He's only thirty-five, and he's a good-looking guy with what sounds like a lucrative job and two young children. He clearly lacks a little confidence, which might suggest why he is paying for a date instead of going on a more natural one, but in reality, a guy like him should have the world at his feet. Instead, he's sitting here in this wine bar with me, sipping nervously from his glass and fumbling around for the next topic of conversation.

I guess I'm not the only one struggling to get my life in order.

As he places his drink back on the table, I take the opportunity to glance at my mobile phone resting on my thigh. I removed it from my handbag as I sat down and strategically placed it on my leg where it is out of sight from Greg but where I am able to keep an eye on it. It's important that I do because I am supposed to stick to a strict timetable. This date is to last two hours and not a minute less. That is the amount of time that Greg has paid the agency for, so that is the time I am obligated to be here for. It's at my discretion if I wish for the date to continue for longer than that, but I can't end it any sooner. That is unless Greg becomes physically threatening towards me, which I deem to be highly unlikely based on how he has been with me so far. He looks like he wouldn't hurt a fly, never mind another human being, and his nervousness at this situation is endearing, if a little sad. I doubt he ever expected to be in this kind of situation and especially not after he got married. Yet here he is, back on the scrapheap of life, desperately seeking company and willing to pay just to have it.

I'm not sure exactly how much he is paying the agency for this two-hour date tonight, but I know that I am making £200 out of it, so they must be getting more. It's crazy to think that Greg and many other men like him are willing to pay hundreds of pounds just for a date with a pretty woman, but from what I've read about online, there are men who are paying in the thousands to do the same thing. Of course, most of the people paying that much for an escort are expecting a little more than some polite conversation over a glass of wine. They want sex, either in their own home or in a hotel room. But I have made it clear with the agency that I am not willing to go down that route. A date in a bar, restaurant or theatre is all the clients will be getting out of me, and I'm told many men on the agency's books are happy for that to be the case.

I glance around at a few of the other couples at the adjacent tables and wonder if any of them realise that this date is not as it seems. But nobody is looking at us, and anybody who does will probably just assume from our nervous body language that we are on a first date and not in the early stages of a professional business transaction. I wonder if anybody else in this bar tonight is here for the same reasons as Greg and I.

Is anybody else here as desperate as we are?

While I have no idea why Greg seems to think that the only way to get a woman to go on a date with him involves forking out a large chunk of cash, my desperation stems from my worrying lack of money. I've been struggling to build myself back up ever since Johnny cleared out my bank account. I still have my office job in London, but with how little I have left over from that wage at the end of the month, it's taking an awfully long time for me to get my balance looking healthy again.

It wouldn't be such a problem if I at least enjoyed my day job and could tolerate the commute, but I can't. I hate every single second of it, and I've had enough. My dream of being a writer hasn't left me, but every day that goes by without me pursuing it leaves me feeling like it is less likely to ever happen.

So here I am entering the world of escorting in order to make as much money as I can in as short a time as possible so I can leave my nine-to-five life behind and finally do what I want to do. That means having to now work several evenings after I've already done a full day in the office. This is my first time escorting, and while I'm uncomfortable so far, I can't afford to screw this up. Without the extra cash from this job, I will never get to achieve my goals.

I'm just about to ask Greg about his favourite holiday destinations, which was one of the topics that was suggested to me by the agency to make conversation, when I feel the buzzing on my leg. I look down and see my phone vibrating. Somebody is calling me.

It's Louise.

'I'm so sorry,' I say, picking up my phone. 'I have an urgent call, and I really have to take this. Is that okay? We can make the time back up at the end. I promise.'

Greg graciously allows me to leave the table, and I rush towards the doors with my phone in my hand, wondering why my daughter is calling me now. If it was anybody else, then I wouldn't have bothered picking up, but Louise never calls me unless she needs something, so I'd better see what it is.

I step out on the street and wait until the glass doors have closed behind me before I accept the call because I want to make sure that the sounds of the busy bar are trapped inside. I told Louise I was going to be working late at the office, so I can hardly answer the phone to the sound of chinking glasses and boisterous laughter.

'Hey! Is everything okay?' I ask.

'Where are you?' comes the gruff reply from the other end of the line.

'I'm working late. I told you I would be.'

'Oh.'

She obviously wasn't listening when I told her. *That's my daughter.*

'What's wrong?' I ask.

'Nothing. I'm just starving, and there's nothing in to eat.'

'There's plenty in,' I reply, but then I'm suddenly not so sure about that. It has been five days since I did a food shop. That's a lot of time for a ravenous teenager to raid the cupboards.

'There isn't. I'm starving,' Louise moans.

'Well, you're a big girl. I'm sure you can find something,' I tell her, moving quickly away from the door to the wine bar as a young couple leave and allow all the noise inside to temporarily escape.

'Can I use your card to get a takeaway?' Louise asks.

'No, I told you we can't afford it. You will have to eat what's in the flat.'

'But I just told you there's nothing in the flat!'

I grip the phone tightly as I feel my blood pressure rising. Why must my daughter always be so difficult? There is probably food in the flat. It might not be exciting, but there will be something to eat. I refuse to believe that we are out of everything. What Louise means when she says there is nothing in is that she is too lazy to cook anything for herself. Instead, she'd rather I just get her a takeaway. But I've told her no more. It's a waste of money, and it all adds up. The more I splurge on things like that, the less likely it is that I will ever get to quit my job, and the more likely it is that I'll have to do the kind of work I'm doing tonight instead.

'No,' I tell her. 'You're not having a takeaway.'

'Pleeeeaassse.'

The easy thing to do would be to give in and just give her my card details so she can order one. But it's been a long time since I did the easy thing.

'No. Eat what's in the flat. I'll be home by ten.'

Then I hang up and head back into the bar. I don't feel bad for saying no to my daughter because it is the right thing to do. The fact she is calling me again as I make my way back to the table in the corner only stiffens my resolve. We're probably going to have a massive argument when I get back home later tonight because of this, but so be it. If she had any idea how hard I was actually working to earn my money, then maybe she would be more understanding. But she doesn't because Louise doesn't understand anything about hard work and earning money. She just thinks it grows on trees. Well, it doesn't. I really wish it did. Maybe then I wouldn't have to be sitting down at this table again and asking Greg if he's enjoying the expensive bottle of wine he just paid for.

'An escort? You? Don't take this the wrong way, but I can't see it.'

I have just finished telling the man opposite me about my extracurricular activities to earn more cash, but I can already see it was a mistake. I was hoping that my confession would garner a little sympathy for me and show him that I'm more than just some office drone who has saved up a portion of her wages over the years. Rather, I am a hard-working mother determined to do anything to better my life. But he just keeps laughing at me.

'So that's how you saved up so much money. People paid to go on a date with you,' he says, shaking his head in amusement. 'Are there really that many desperate men in the world?'

'They weren't desperate. They were just lonely,' I correct him.

'Whatever. I can't get over the fact that you were an escort.'

'Why not?'

'Aren't escorts supposed to be all glamorous?'

I'd be more offended by the statement if it hadn't come after all the threats to me and my daughter. Instead, my level of hate for this man can't get any higher than it already is right now.

'I had a disguise,' I tell him, referring to the blonde wig I used to put on.

'Well, it must have been a bloody good one because I still can't see it working, I'm afraid.'

'Fuck you,' I tell him, and this time it's my turn to stubbornly cross my arms.

'Did you, you know…' he says suggestively.

'No, I did not,' I reply firmly, knowing exactly what he is referring to.

He takes a moment to enjoy the hatred coming at him across the table before shrugging his shoulders.

'Okay, I admit it. You were right. There is more to you than meets the eye,' he says with an appreciative nod of the head. 'But that doesn't change anything. So you made your money as an escort. So what? That money is still going to be mine by the time we get to Brighton.'

I watch him check the time on his watch again as I feel the train slowing as we make our approach to the next station. Several passengers take out their headphones, close their newspapers or put away their phones and go through the tedious routine of gathering up their belongings in preparation to disembark.

I watch a couple of them, including an elderly woman in a business suit who moves slowly and looks exhausted. She looks to be in her mid-sixties. Retirement age. She should be enjoying herself at her age, not clinging on to the back of her seat for balance as the train sways while she attempts to reach her coat in the overhead storage area. I wonder why she is still commuting. The obvious answer is that she still needs the money, but she looks old enough to be drawing a pension. Unless of course, she is one of the unfortunate ones who got screwed by the government when they changed the age of entitlement. There is a woman in my office who suffered the same fate. She could have retired at sixty, but she has fallen into the group that must work until they are sixty-five now through no fault of her own. She isn't happy about it, and she isn't the only one. There have been petitions, protests, and plenty of pleading with the powers that be about allowing those unlucky workers who had the goalposts moved on them to retire earlier, but they have all gone unheard. *Keep working. There's no escape.*

Not yet.

I notice the woman is struggling to remove her coat from the overhead space. It seems to have been trapped beneath a heavy briefcase, and I'm just about to offer my help when my tormentor offers his instead.

'Let me get that for you.'

He gets up from his seat and lends his assistance to the passenger, lifting up the briefcase and allowing the woman to pull her coat out more easily. I'm surprised to see the show of chivalry from the man who is currently trying to extort money out of me, as well as being dismayed to see that he has kept his phone in his hand as he does it.

'Thank you,' the woman says as she pulls on her coat as he retakes his seat.

'No problem at all,' he says with a wide smile that I would just love to wipe off his face.

Then the woman turns to me before she departs. 'You've got yourself a good one there,' she says, beaming at us both before shuffling away towards the doors and out onto the platform.

I didn't get a chance to correct her and tell her that I'm not actually with this man, nor is he as gentlemanly as he appears, but she is gone, disappearing with everybody else who disembarked at the same time.

The train is much quieter now, and most of the seats are available as the doors close, and we set off again on the penultimate part of the journey. I don't need him to tell me that we are now only eighteen minutes from Brighton.

As the train passes along the platform, I notice that the large grin on his face is still there. He seems rather proud of himself for what he has just done.

'See. I'm not all bad.'

'I guess that was your one good deed for the day,' I reply sarcastically.

'No. There is still plenty of time for one more. I can give your daughter the gift of life. You only have to say the magic words. Or rather, the magic numbers.'

He holds up his phone again to remind me that all of this could potentially be over with a simple call to his partner, but that's not what I'm thinking about right now. I'm thinking about if I have any chance of grabbing that phone from his hand and running down the carriage before he can catch up with me.

Probably not.

Why would that work when everything else has gone wrong for me?

'So you really didn't sleep with any of those men?' he asks me suddenly.

'I told you I didn't.'

'Not even one? A favourite client perhaps? There must have been at least one guy you actually liked.'

I shake my head to tell him that I did not sleep with any of the men who paid me for a date. But I did have a favourite client once upon a time. We went on several dates together, and he was a pleasant and charming man.

That was until he turned out to be exactly like the rest of the men in my life.

24

ONE MONTH EARLIER

Another night. Another wine bar. But this date is different.

This is going to be my last one.

I'm already seated at the table, and I was actually a few minutes early tonight, which tells me that the nerves I felt when I first started doing this work six months ago have dissipated somewhat. There have still been awkward dates for sure, and there are still plenty of times when I feel like my client is going to tell me this was a mistake and demand a refund, but those have mostly been replaced now by the sense that I am doing a decent job.

I'm friendly and polite. I'm a capable conversationalist. And I look reasonably good, as a quick check on my reflection in the mirror behind the bar confirms.

I've even got used to the blonde wig on my head.

I possess all the things I need to be a good escort and

satisfy my clients. Of course, there have been a few of them who wanted more than a nice chat over a couple of drinks and tried to tempt me back to various hotel rooms with offers of even more money. But I always turned them down. There's a fine line between what I do and what a prostitute does. I make sure I stay on the right side of it.

Besides, it's not as if I'm desperate for money these days. Since I began this unorthodox way of earning cash, I've managed to accrue quite the nest egg. I'm not rich by any means. I never have been, and I doubt I ever will be, well, not unless my book actually gets published, but that would require me to finish it first. But for the first time in my life, I'm no longer just getting by. I actually have proper savings now and much more than the five grand I had when my ex-boyfriend took it from my account. I have almost £20,000, a big chunk of it gained in the line of work that I am engaging in this evening, and all of it currently kept locked away in the small safe back at my flat.

The reason for the safe is because of my distrust of the bank after the way they treated me in the wake of Johnny cleaning out my account. They took no responsibility for allowing him to transfer the funds and blamed the whole thing on me for not being more careful with who saw my personal details. I went into the bank on several occasions and demanded better answers from them, but I left after a massive argument every single time. Ever since then, I decided that I would not trust anybody else with my money.

I work hard to make it.

I'm going to work even harder to keep it.

With that in mind, I purchased a small safe online and stored it in the bottom of my wardrobe, using it to deposit the part of my wages I withdraw from the cash machine each month. That was my backup plan in case anything ever happened with the bank again, but when I started escorting, it became a great way of keeping all my extra money off the books.

The agency offered to pay me in cash, and I gratefully accepted. No tax means higher profits, and it hasn't taken long to start filling up that safe with stacks of fifty-pound notes. My goal was to reach £20,000 before I quit my job, and after the payment from tonight's date, I will have made it. Tomorrow, I will walk into my office and hand in my one month's notice, and then the countdown will begin to the day when I will become a full-time writer.

I'm hoping I'll never have to go back to work, but if I do, it's good to know that this opportunity exists in the escorting world. I wouldn't say I enjoy it, but it's far easier than an eight-hour grind in the office. Drink some wine. Laugh at some bad jokes. Get paid.

If it weren't for my love of writing, I'd probably just be an escort forever.

Or at least until I was no longer pretty enough to get clients.

I check the time on my phone, which I still position on my leg underneath the table during dates so I can discreetly keep an eye on how long is left. As I do, I notice that my date for this evening is running late. That is very unusual for any client, let alone this particular one. Not many people are late to an appointment for which they are paying by the hour, and especially not at these prices. But a quick glance around the bar tells me that my date is still not here.

Oh well, I'll just wait.

I scroll through my phone to pass the time and notice a social media update from my daughter as I do. She is asking her followers for the best places to visit in

Asia. She is obviously still determined to go backpacking, I see.

I notice that she has already received several comments, most of which are telling her to visit Bali and some beach called Pandawa. It certainly sounds exotic and much more so than the place where I took Louise for her last holiday.

We went to Clacton-on-Sea.

There weren't many backpackers there.

I'm tempted to write a snarky comment asking her if she has found a job to fund this Asia trip, but I decide it's best not to. I get into enough arguments with my daughter when it's just the two of us. There's no point starting one in full view of everybody on social media.

I lock my phone again and return it to its usual place on my leg before taking a sip from the glass of water that the waiter kindly poured for me when I sat down. As I do, I think about my daughter and wonder if I am being too harsh on her. I told her that I wouldn't be giving her the money to go travelling and that she would have to get a job to save up for it if she was really serious about it. Of course, Louise didn't like that and told me that I should give her the money as a present for finishing school last year. I told her that I couldn't afford it, but she disagreed. I wondered how she could do that, but then she told me she knew about my safe.

Apparently, she had seen it in the bottom of my wardrobe when she had sneaked in there to borrow one of my tops the day before. The sight of it seemed to confirm to her that I was sitting on a small fortune. I tried to pretend that there was nothing in the safe except for my passport and a few important banking documents, but Louise didn't buy it. I might have raised a stubborn and argumentative child, but I didn't raise a fool. She told me she knew there was money in there, and my face gave away the fact that it was true.

I tried to explain to her that the incident with Johnny had left me distrustful of the bank, so the safe had seemed like a good idea. I told her that I had been given a pay rise at work and been saving hard over the last few months, which she seemed to buy as a cover story, sparing me having to tell her the truth that her mother had been going on dates with wealthy men four nights a week. But her knowledge of the cash only made her more determined that I should give her some money.

The fact I told her the money was for my writing went down about as well as expected.

'Amanda, I'm so sorry I'm late.'

I hear the distressed voice of the old man just over my shoulder and turn around to see my date smiling down at me. 'Charles, lovely to see you!' I say as I get up out of my seat and go to give him a hug.

I am not usually so affectionate with clients, but this one is different from all the others. Charles is much older than the rest of them, for a start. He's seventy-one, with wisps of grey hair on his head and a posture that tells me he is weary from a lifetime of working hard. He's also the only client I have who isn't single because of divorce. Charles is a widow. His wife, Mary, passed away five years ago, and after one too many lonely nights at home, he has entered the world of escorting to give himself a little company in his twilight years.

I've never felt emotionally attached to any of the men I have shared a meal or a bottle of wine with over the last six months, except this man standing in front of me right now with his diminutive frame drowning in an oversized suit. He looks so cute, and it breaks my heart to think that he is dressing up to impress me now because he is no longer able to do it for the woman he truly loved.

I shed several tears on our previous dates when he recalled his last few days with his wife before she died, and I also felt the fear of the future gripping me when he talked about what it is like to be alone at his age with no one to even talk to. All he wants is some company to share his many stories with, and ever since we met, I have been more than happy to provide it for him.

I have been on several dates with Charles over the last few months, most of them in this bar right here, but a couple at the theatre just around the corner. Charles loves the performing arts and used to watch several plays a month with his wife before she passed. While I could never come close to replacing her, I was more than happy to take her place and sit beside him in those dark rooms while we watched the actors entertain us on the stage. But it was only after a couple of these dates when Charles confessed to being more than a fan of the theatre, telling me that he actually used to work in it.

His eyes came alive as he recalled his varied career as a director for several productions in the West End, and I was thrilled to hear all about his time spent working with some of the most famous actors and actresses in the country. But it was only when I got home and put his name into Google that I actually saw how famous he was in his own right. Far from being just a pleasant man, Charles was also one of the most successful theatre directors this country has ever produced.

But putting his impressive and illustrious career aside, I'm going to miss this man after tonight simply because he makes me feel good. He is full of warmth, humour, and good grace, as well as possessing some of the finest manners I have ever seen a man display—it's not an exaggeration to say that he has restored my faith in the male population.

If only he were thirty years younger.

But the thought of saying goodbye to Charles makes me anxious because I know he won't be expecting it. I still need to break the news to him that I won't be able to go on any more dates after this one tonight, and that will be difficult. The sight of the colourful flowers in his hand only makes it even more so.

'I got these for you,' Charles says, holding out the bouquet of purple lilies towards me. 'It's why I was so late. I was trying to find a good bunch.'

'You didn't have to do that!' I say, accepting the flowers. 'They're beautiful!'

I mean it. They really are. I can't believe he remembered what my favourite flowers are. I only mentioned it in passing, and it must have been several weeks ago when I did.

'Beautiful flowers for a beautiful lady,' Charles says, and then he proceeds to pull out my chair a little more from the table. 'Please, after you.'

I graciously accept the offer of a seat as Charles slowly removes his smart dinner jacket and goes to hang it on the back of his chair.

The waiter who served me my water is quickly on hand to ask if Charles would like to put his jacket in the cloakroom, but I already know what the response will be. Charles will say no because he had an experience where his coat went missing once, and he was rather upset about that because his wife had bought it for him.

'No, thank you,' Charles tells the waiter politely but firmly. 'But could we have some water for the flowers, please?'

'Of course, sir.'

The waiter scurries away as Charles eases himself

into his seat, and I smile at this pleasant man as I hold onto the flowers while awaiting the water.

'So how have you been, my dear?' he asks me, his left hand trembling slightly as he fiddles with the button on his shirtsleeve.

'I've been very well, thank you,' I reply, noticing his struggle with the button but making sure not to let him see that I have. He is a very proud man, and I know he likes to think of himself as still being younger than his years give away.

During our dates, I have noticed that he seems to go through spells where he is surprisingly spritely but then fairly frail. I feel as if being around him is witnessing the body's constant battle with itself as it descends into old age and can no longer do the things that used to come so easily to it. It's sad to see, but it will happen to us all, I suppose.

Not for the first time since being around Charles, I think about my own mortality and what it will be like to grow old alone. While Charles had his love life cut tragically short by his wife's passing, I have no such excuse. The only dates I have been on recently have been the professional kind where I am getting paid for it. Maybe it's time for me to do something about that. Charles has already told me that it's a shame for a pretty woman like me to be going to bed alone every night, and I understand what he means, even if I was a little surprised to hear him say it. He was letting me know that I deserve company, and to fall asleep beside the person I love before waking up in their arms and looking forward to a new day with them. I know that I do want that too, even after I have been hurt so many times, and even after what my last boyfriend did to me. But for now, I am focused on myself and my career. I am going to be a writer. That is the goal. But being with Charles reminds me that there is more to life than just personal ambitions.

It isn't much of a life without love.

As the waiter returns to our table with a vase of water for my flowers, I feel bad that I'm going to be putting a stop to these dates with Charles after this evening. I will have to break the news gently, but I will tell him the truth. He knows that this is just a job for me, and he knows about my big plans, so I doubt he will begrudge me pursuing them. But I expect he will be a little sad to no longer have our dates to look forward to, and I will be too. He has told me that it took him a long time to pluck up the courage to even try escorting and that he wouldn't want to do it if I stopped. Sadly, that is what I am going to do.

But we can enjoy a few glasses of wine before I tell him that.

25

The sound of the can being cracked open behind me snaps me out of my daydream, and I turn around to see a guy two rows behind me sipping a cheap lager. While I'm not a fan of his drink of choice, I don't begrudge him a drink on his way home this evening. I went through a little spell where I used to have a can of gin and tonic on my way home every night, but I put a stop to it when one can turned into two and it became the only highlight of my day.

'Thirsty?'

I turn back around and look at the man at my table.

'No,' I reply.

'I am,' he tells me. 'I'm looking forward to a beer when all of this is over. Which reminds me, you've only got fifteen minutes left before time is up and Louise pays for your stubbornness.'

He taps his watch again, but it's his phone I am looking at.

I am praying he lets go of it again.

'If I'm honest, I'm surprised you have lasted this long,' he says to me, sitting forward again. 'I think most mums would have just given up the code the second they found out their child was in danger.'

'Why should I give in so easily?' I fire back, and the man shrugs.

'I don't know. Maybe because my partner is going to gut your daughter like a fish if you don't.'

I know it's a risky strategy, but I decide to try it. I'm going to call his bluff. At least if I can distract him, he might forget about his phone for a minute.

'I don't think he has it in him,' I say, doing my best to stay calm as I speak. 'I think the pair of you are all talk.'

'Really?'

'Yes. I think you believed that me and my daughter would be easy marks and just roll over and give you what you wanted. But we aren't like that. We're fighters. We've never had anything given to us. We've had to scrap for everything we have. Our home. Our money. Our lives.'

'Please,' he says, waving his hand in the air dismissively. 'If you're going to try to convince me that you two are anything more than just a couple of average women living in an average town, then you can forget about it.'

I'm so angry, and I wish I could let him know who I really was and what I have done. Maybe then he would think twice about what he is doing. But I can't. It would be too dangerous to do that. But then again, he's going to find out anyway if I don't do something soon.

'I want you to listen to me now,' I say, sitting forward in my seat. 'I want you to realise that you are getting yourself involved in something much bigger than you realise. This isn't just about money. It's more than that.'

'And I want you to realise that I don't care,' he replies with a shrug.

'You will do. Trust me. If you open that safe, you will be making a big mistake.'

'Why is that?'

'I've already proven to you that there are some things about me that you didn't know.'

'And?'

'So what else is there that I might be hiding? What else have you missed in all the time you were watching me?'

I let him dwell on that for a moment until he ultimately gives up.

'What?' he asks, clearly frustrated.

But this is what I want. I need him to lose his air of calm because if I can get him on edge, he is more likely to make a mistake that gives me a chance to get out of this.

'That's my point,' I say. 'You have no idea. You can't possibly fathom what I have done in my past to get to this point, nor can you fathom what I am willing to do to protect what I have. So with that in mind, why don't you just walk away? Before it's too late.'

He holds eye contact with me as he processes what I have just said, and I imagine he is trying to see if I will break first, but I don't. I stare right back and let him know that I'm not afraid of him. Rather, he should be the one who is afraid of me.

It's a pleasant surprise when he is the one who looks away, and he does so to check his watch again. Then he unlocks his phone again.

'What are you doing?' I ask.

'You'll see,' he says, putting his mobile to his ear.

I look out of the window at the green fields rushing by as the train continues hurtling towards the coast. We're not that far away now, and I usually feel optimistic when we reach this point because the end of my day is almost in sight.

But not today.

'James, we're going to have to speed things up a little here,' he says into his phone. 'Take off one of her toes.'

He didn't really say that, did he?

'No!' I cry, lunging across the table towards him. But he ducks out of the way and manages to keep the phone to his ear.

'Don't hurt her! Please!' I beg, terrified now that I have played this all wrong, and my daughter is going to pay for it.

'What's the code?' he asks me again as I continue to try to grab his mobile but to no avail.

'Leave her alone! Please!'

He shakes his head. 'He's just gone getting a knife from your kitchen,' he tells me with an evil grin on his face.

'No. Please!' I beg, but I think I'm too late when he puts his phone on speaker and tells me to listen to what's happening back at my flat.

That's when I hear Louise's screams from the other end of the line.

26

LOUISE

'No! Please!' I cry as James holds his mobile out towards me with one hand while moving the knife in his other hand in the direction of my feet. 'Stop it! Please, I'm begging you!'

I wriggle on the bed and do my best to keep my feet away from the edge of the blade, but there's only so much I can do with my hands tied above my head.

'Help me! Help!'

James puts the phone down on the bed as he grabs my left foot and brings the knife nearer, and I realise I'm not going to be able to prevent this. The fact he has put this whole awful ordeal on speakerphone so my mum can presumably listen in makes it even worse.

'You're sick!' I hiss at the man at the bottom of the bed as he puts the knife to my skin, but it's going to happen now whatever I do, so I close my eyes and wait for the pain to come. Hopefully, it won't be as bad as I imagine it to be. But he's going to cut one of my toes off.

How can it not be bad?

I grit my teeth and keep my eyes clamped shut to

avoid the sight of the blood spurting across the bottom of the bed, but then nothing happens.

There's no pain. There's no blood. When I open my eyes, I see that there's not even a knife by my feet anymore. Instead, James is smiling at me.

'Don't worry. You can keep your toes for now. We're just scaring your mum. I'm pretty sure that will have done the trick.'

I feel my chest rising and falling fast, and my heart rate must be off the charts as I try to come to terms with what almost happened to me. But my fear is quickly replaced by something else.

Anger.

Without warning, I slam my foot straight into James's face, sending him sprawling backwards on to the carpet from where he was crouching at the bottom of the bed.

He lets out a howl of pain, and it feels good for a split second. It feels even better when I see him get to his feet and catch sight of the amount of blood pouring from his nose.

'You stupid bitch!' he cries, and for a second it looks like I am going to seriously pay for my one brief moment of revenge. There is still a knife in here somewhere, after all, and I'm still tied up.

But then he rushes from the room, and I hear him go into the bathroom, so I can at least relax for a moment. He is probably checking his damaged nose in the mirror.

If only I could get out of these restraints before he comes back.

I wriggle my wrists again, and the cable tie digs into my skin, causing me to grimace in pain. It's not quite as bad as having a toe cut off, but it's still not great.

'Come on!' I cry in frustration as I shake my wrists

and do my best to stretch my restraints away from the bedpost. This bedframe might look sturdy, but I know it isn't as strong as it appears because I almost broke it once by jumping on it. It was only the fact that Mum dragged me off it that stopped me from causing any real damage, but I remember how she told me how fragile it actually was and that she couldn't afford to buy a new one if it broke.

But unlike then, I have to put my own selfish needs above money, so I keep pulling and wriggling my arms, putting as much force against the bedpost as I can. If I almost broke this bed once, then surely I can break it now.

Then I hear a crack.

I'm just about to pull again when I hear James walk back into the room, and I stop, desperate not to give away the fact that I was potentially only a few seconds from escape.

I can feel the slack in my restraints from the damaged bedpost and know that I could have snapped it off completely if I had kept going. But I don't want James to see. I'll do it when he isn't looking. But right now, he is staring at me with a bloody face.

'You'd better pray your mum gives us that code, or I swear to God I'm going to enjoy killing you,' he says as he holds a tissue over his nose to stem the bleeding.

'Just let me go!' I try again even though I know it won't do me any good.

James says nothing as he continues to treat his injury, and I'm hoping he just goes back into the bathroom, but he remains standing by the bottom of the bed for the moment, which means my chances at making a run for it are reduced. I'll never get past him if I try now. But if he's in the bathroom, I could make it to the door before him. I'm just praying I get that chance. That's because I've realised it is my only chance now.

My mum has made it pretty clear that she isn't willing to give up her money to save my life. If she wanted to do it, then all of this could have been over with by now. She could have given up the code, allowed James to open the safe, and now he would have left, leaving me safe instead of still in a perilous position. But if she hasn't done it yet, I doubt she ever will. How much more persuading does she need? I almost lost a body part, and I might lose a lot more than that if the look on James's face is anything to go by.

I can't believe Mum is allowing this to happen.

I always thought she hated me.

But I didn't realise she hated me this much.

27

AMANDA

I have my head in my hands and tears in my eyes, and I can't bring myself to look at the man sitting opposite me. He has just allowed me to listen to my daughter being attacked by his partner at the flat, and I'll never get the sounds of her desperate cries for help out of my head now.

This is all my fault. Louise would have been counting on me to save her, and I've let her down because I thought there was a way out of this that wouldn't involve me giving up the code to that safe. But I was a fool for thinking like that. No matter what I have done in my past and what secrets I am trying to keep hidden, these men are clearly more dangerous than me.

'Okay, I'll give you the code,' I say, feeling utterly defeated.

'Finally,' he replies, and he holds his phone in anticipation to send the sequence of numbers that I am about to give him.

I take a deep breath and go for it. 'It's 257—'

'Good evening. Sorry to trouble you both, but I'm

raising money for disadvantaged youths in Brighton, and I was wondering if you would be so kind as to donate? It's a very good cause, and we have helped hundreds of youngsters so far, including many young children who are—'

I look at the young man standing by our table in his bright yellow bib with a white bucket in hand, and even in my distressed state, I feel touched to see someone like him trying to raise money for a good cause. He looks to be around Louise's age, but unlike most teenagers I know, he is actually doing something productive with his time.

'Not right now,' my harasser says, cutting the fundraiser off quickly.

'Oh. Okay. How about you, miss? Could you spare a little change? It really is for a good cause. I'm raising funds for a new youth centre where youngsters who don't have any support can go in the evenings after school. I actually spent a lot of time in one myself when I was growing up, but the council closed it down, unfortunately.'

'I said no!' the man says again, this time with more venom in his voice, and the fundraiser gets the message this time and goes to leave.

But I put a hand out to stop him because I don't want him to leave yet, although it's not because I feel bad for him.

It's because he might be the distraction that I need to get my hands on that phone.

'I can give you something,' I say, reaching into my handbag and pulling out my purse. 'I'll give you twenty pounds if my friend here gives you something too. How does that sound?'

The fundraiser smiles. 'That sounds very generous. Thank you!'

I smile at the young man and turn to the less pleasant one sitting at my table.

'You heard me. Get your money out,' I tell him as I unzip my purse.

'We don't have time for this,' he replies, but I shrug my shoulders.

'I've changed my mind about what we were talking about. Unless you donate too, I won't give you what you want.'

I notice the puzzled look on the fundraiser's face, but I ignore it and watch the man opposite.

Is he going to go along with this?

'Fine, whatever,' he says, and he reaches into his pocket to get his wallet out. But as he does, he puts his phone down on the table, and that is the chance I need.

Quick as a flash, I grab his device and leap up out of my seat, running down the carriage before he can grab hold of me.

'Hey!' he calls after me, and I turn back to see him pushing his way past the confused fundraiser and chasing after me. But I have a good head start on him, and I'm already at the doors to the next carriage.

I push the button, and they slide open automatically, allowing me to run through. I see a few people dotted around in their seats as I race past them, and it's a little busier in this carriage than it was on mine. Fortunately, everybody is sitting down, so the aisle is free for me to move along.

I spot the sign for the toilets up ahead and keep going, praying that I can make it there and lock the door before he catches up with me. To find out if that is realistic, I turn around to see where he is and spot him coming through the doors behind me.

He is definitely closing on me. But I'm going to make it.

At least I am right up until the moment when I slip on something.

The sudden loss of my footing causes the phone to fly out of my hand and hit the floor of the carriage. I look behind me to see what caused my fall and spot the discarded newspaper lying in the aisle. I slipped on it, and several of the pages have scattered around, now lying on the floor around me.

Then I feel the hand on my shoulder.

It must be him.

He's caught me.

Now it's over.

But then I look up and see the concerned face of a middle-aged woman. It's just a fellow passenger checking if I am okay and trying to help me back to my feet. He hasn't caught up with me yet.

But he will any moment now.

I'm just about to climb back to my feet to retrieve the phone when I notice the photo on one of the pages of the newspaper. It's a picture that accompanies one of the articles.

It's a man I recognise.

It's the man whose face I will never forget.

28

AMANDA

ONE MONTH EARLIER

My last date as an escort is almost over. Charles and I have enjoyed a lovely bottle of wine and some good conversation in this classy wine bar in West London, but now it's time for the moment I've been nervously putting off.

I'm going to tell him that I won't be seeing him again.

I feel bad because I know he will be disappointed. He clearly enjoys my company, even with the age difference between us, and we have found plenty of things in common during our dates. I assumed most men who paid for an escort without the promise of sex at the end were doing it because they were lonely and just needed somebody to talk to, and Charles is no different. But what does make him different from all the other men I have sat across the table from in places like this over the last few months is that he doesn't have time on his side like they do. Those men are still young, and they will probably remarry. But Charles has made it clear that he doesn't want to remarry after the loss of his wife and that if it weren't for the service that the agency provides, he would be alone every night in his apartment with nothing but photos of the past to keep him company.

I don't want to upset him, but I have to break the news to him myself; otherwise he will hear that I have left when he calls the agency again to arrange another date, and that's not fair. I should be the one to tell him. That way we can say our proper goodbyes.

I take a large gulp of my red wine and prepare to get it over with.

Here we go.

But just before I speak, Charles reaches into his jacket pocket and removes an envelope from inside. Then he slides it across the table towards me.

'What is it?' I ask, not wanting to pick it up yet because whatever it is, it surely can't help make what I am about to do any easier.

'Open it,' Charles says with his charming smile, and I do as he says as he takes another glug of his wine.

I reach into the envelope and pull out two tickets. Turning them over, I see they are for a performance of *Chicago* at a theatre in Covent Garden.

'Your favourite show,' Charles says, placing his wine glass carefully back down on the table. 'I thought we could go for our next date. There's a performance next Tuesday. I checked with the agency beforehand, and they said you were free.'

It's a thoughtful gesture, and I'm touched by the generosity, as well as the fact that he remembered my favourite show from our discussion a few weeks ago, but this isn't helping me say goodbye.

'Thank you, Charles. This is very kind,' I say, sliding the tickets back into the envelope. 'But I'm afraid I'm going to have to decline. I'm so sorry.'

I see the disappointment on Charles's face instantly, and I feel terrible. Why couldn't my last date as an escort be with some sexist pig who drinks too much and chews food with his mouth open? Instead, it's with one of the most charming, friendly and sensitive men I have ever met.

They certainly don't make them like Charles anymore, that's for sure.

'Oh, that's a pity,' he says, lowering his eyes to the tablecloth. 'Have I made a mistake?'

'No, not at all,' I quickly reply, reaching out and gently resting my hand on his own on the table.

I know the people at the agency advised against any physical contact during dates in case it gave the wrong impression, but I'm making an exception for Charles because he is so sweet, and I don't want him to feel like I don't care about his feelings. He looks like he could burst into tears at any moment, and that would kill me.

'It's just that I'm not going to be available anymore for these dates,' I tell him. 'I'm leaving the agency. I'm going to have a go at being a writer full time. Like I discussed, remember?'

I hope that adding in the part about me pursuing my dream will soften the blow for him and lead to him being excited for me rather than just feeling sorry for himself. That way we can both toast to our future endeavours and then be on our way. But the look on Charles's face lets me know that he isn't excited.

He is crushed.

He removes his hand from under mine and picks up the envelope before tucking it back into his jacket pocket.

'Are you okay?' I ask, genuinely worried.

'I'm fine,' he tells me as he checks his watch. 'It's almost nine. You can leave if you like.'

I know he is telling me that because nine o'clock is the time when our date is scheduled to end, and he presumably thinks I just want to get home and get on with what I'd rather be doing. But he's wrong. I enjoy our dates together, even though they are a business transaction, and that is evidenced by the fact that I didn't realise it was late already. The time we spent chatting has just flown by. Then I'm reminded that we did start the date a little after the scheduled start time because Charles was running late.

He was running late because he had stopped to buy me flowers.

'Charles, I want you to know that I've enjoyed our evenings together, and I probably shouldn't say this, but you were my favourite client.'

I know I definitely shouldn't have said that because that was another thing that the agency told me not to do. Apparently, an escort telling a client that they are their favourite can lead to them forming strong emotional attachments that can prove difficult to break. But I think it's already too late for that in this case. I can see that because it looks like Charles has a tear in his eye.

He wipes it away quickly before I can say another word, and it's not long until his fragile demeanour has been replaced by a stiff upper lip and a dogged determination to carry on.

'To the future,' he says, raising his glass of wine in the air.

I smile at him and pick up my own drink, pleased to see that we are going to be able to end our arrangement on good terms after all.

'To the future.'

It's ten minutes later when we step outside the busy bar, and I thank Charles as he holds the door open for me. A true gentleman until the end, that is how I will remember him.

I'm glad we are ending things on a positive note, and I'm just about to say goodbye and take out my phone to book a taxi to the station when I notice that he is looking rather forlorn again.

'I'm tired of being alone,' he says to me softly, and my heart breaks in that moment as I look at him.

'Oh, Charles, you're not alone,' I say, putting my hand on his arm and feeling his thin bones through his thick jacket. 'You have your family, right? Your daughter. The grandchildren. And what about your friends? There's Bill and Andrew at the billiards club, yeah?'

I recall the people that he has told me about in the past, doing my best to remind him that he is not as lonely as he thinks he is. But it doesn't seem to work. Charles looks no happier.

'That's not what I mean. I miss my Mary. I miss having somebody to talk to in the evenings when I'm sitting at home. I miss playing a record for her and reading the paper while she potters around me. I miss it all.'

I always knew how much Charles was pining after his late wife, because he has brought her up on every single one of our dates. But unlike those other occasions where he would only reminisce about the happier memories like their holidays overseas or their times spent raising a family, now it seems he is focusing on the negatives. It's the negative of never getting to be with the woman he loves again.

'You don't understand, Amanda. These dates might

have just been work for you, but for me, they have given me a purpose. Something to look forward to when I'm sitting alone all day. It's taken me a long time to find somebody at the agency whom I could trust and who would actually listen to me instead of just humour me. And now you're leaving.'

I feel terrible. *But what can I say?*

'I'm sorry you feel that way, Charles. If there was anything I could do to make you feel better, I would do it, but—'

'Have one more drink with me.'

I'm surprised by the invitation, mainly because we both know our allotted time has come to an end.

'I'm not able to do that, Charles. Agency rules.'

'I'll pay you if that's what you're worried about,' he snaps back, and that only makes me feel worse because I know that he only thinks I am with him for the money. I was at the beginning, but I've gotten to know him since then, and I wish he knew that I saw him as a friend and not just a client these days.

'I don't want your money,' I tell him, and I mean it. I just want to have a civil goodbye and get in a taxi.

'Two thousand pounds,' Charles says.

'Excuse me?'

'I'll give you two thousand pounds if you come for one more drink with me,' Charles says, and the crazy thing is that I can see that he means it.

'No, thank you,' I tell him, even though my mind is swimming with the possibilities of what I could do with that money. Considering I'm planning on quitting my job in the near future and pursuing the unreliable career path of an author, every extra penny would help. But I can't accept the offer. It's too much money, even for somebody as wealthy as him.

'Charles, I think it's best if we just say goodbye,' I say. 'I wish you all the best in the future.'

'I'll give you the cash tonight. Just one drink, that's all I ask. Then we can say goodbye somewhere more comfortable than this street corner.'

I look at the old man standing in front of me, and my heart breaks for him because he didn't ask for any of this. He was happy with his wife until she passed away and left him all alone. Now here he is standing outside a wine bar, throwing money at me just to give him a little more company before I leave him forever.

I check the time on my phone and figure I still have plenty of wiggle room before my last train home. I could stay with him for a little while longer, I suppose.

'Okay, one more drink,' I say, going against my better judgement. 'But you're not paying me. This one is on the house.'

I feel bad enough for this poor man as it is without exploiting him.

'Excellent,' he replies with a beaming smile, and it's clear I've just made his night.

'So where do you want to go?' I ask as I drop my phone back into my handbag.

'My place,' Charles quickly replies, and he turns to walk away.

'Hang on a minute,' I call after him, suddenly regretting my decision to agree. 'I thought we were going to another bar.'

'I didn't say that. I said one more drink somewhere more comfortable. I would like that drink at my apartment.'

This is definitely against all the rules that were explained to me when I joined the escort agency. Never mind no physical contact and not talking about personal issues. The number one rule was do not go back to a client's apartment.

'I can't,' I say to Charles. 'It has to be a public place, or I can't do it.'

Charles thinks about it for a moment, then shrugs.

'Five thousand pounds.'

29

LATER THAT NIGHT

I shouldn't be doing this. I should have said no. But £5,000 is a lot of money, and I'd be a fool to turn it down. I'd have to work for over two months in my office job to earn that. Or I could just have one drink with a lonely old man. Considering I'm preparing to leave my job, how could I turn him down? I can stretch that money out to last me a long time when I'm trying to make it as a struggling writer. So I said yes. I followed Charles home. Now we're in his apartment, and I'm watching him make me a drink.

'So what do you think of the old place?' he asks as he pours me a measure of gin at the impressive mahogany bar he has fitted into his luxurious front room.

'It's amazing,' I admit, shaking my head as I look around at the surroundings.

I can't quite believe I'm in a place like this. It's a palatial three-bedroom apartment in Chelsea, and while

I knew it would be unlike any home I had been in before, I still hadn't been prepared for the sight that met me when I walked through the front door and actually laid eyes on it.

The enormous rooms are filled with the very best furniture money can buy, with garish features like the giant bar, the enormous sauna in the bedroom and the huge hot tub on the balcony.

And the view.

Oh my, the view.

The apartment overlooks the Thames, and from this prime position on the banks of the river, we can see the boats sailing past and the lights twinkling on the water from all the high-rise buildings that line the edge of London's famous inlet.

I dread to think what a place like this must cost, but it's obviously in the millions. No wonder Charles is so flush with his cash. He obviously can afford to be.

It's a far cry from my little flat in Brighton, where Louise and I are constantly tripping over each other's things in our daily battle for space and privacy. But the size of this apartment also makes me feel a little sad because it's far too big for one man to live in alone.

All the money in the world can't bring back his Mary.

I haven't failed to notice the numerous photos around the apartment of Charles and his late wife, all of them taken at various points in their long relationship. There are the black-and-white ones from their younger days, and there are the colour ones in which it's become more evident that time has started to take a toll on their bodies but not on their love for each other.

Charles has pointed out a few of his favourites to me already, including the one of him and Mary beside the Trevi Fountain in Rome. It's clear that all he wants is somebody to reminisce with to fill his long, lonely hours. Ideally, he would find a new partner for that, preferably one closer to his age, but then again, with his money, he could probably attract whoever he wanted. But for the interim, he just needs company tonight, any company, and I'm glad I can provide it for him. The fact I am being paid a ridiculous amount of money to do it is not ideal for my conscience, but I have to remember that I am out tonight because I am working, so it's only right that I earn.

'Here we go,' Charles says as he brings our drinks over and joins me on the sofa.

'Thank you,' I say as I accept the gin and tonic, and I'm just about to take a sip when he stops me.

'We haven't toasted yet,' he reminds me, and I lower my glass.

Charles takes a moment to decide on what it is exactly that we should drink to before fixing me with his warm smile and raising his measure of whiskey.

'To you, Amanda. May you one day sell so many books that you can buy yourself a home like this and be my neighbour.'

I laugh at the toast, but also feel touched that he is still conscious of my dream. Even in his lonely state, he displays such a caring attitude towards others.

We touch glasses before drinking, and I savour the refreshing liquid as it slips down my throat. Having been on red wine for the whole evening, it's nice to have a change of pace, and as I take another sip, I'm not regretting coming back here at all.

'I can't get over how incredible your view is,' I say, marvelling again at the sight of the river flowing by outside.

'Do you have a view in your place?' he asks me, and I laugh, not because the question is ridiculous but because the answer is.

'Yeah, I have a view. I can see the side of the next building if I strain my head out of the bathroom window enough.'

Charles smiles and takes a sip of his whiskey, and I catch a glimpse of the golden wedding band on his fourth finger.

I take a moment to ponder whether I should go ahead and say what's on my mind, and in the end, I decide to go for it because I'm not going to see him after tonight anyway.

'I know you have said that you could never find love again after Mary,' I begin, treading carefully so as not to upset my host. 'But I really think you should at least consider going on a few dates. Proper ones, I mean. Not escorts.'

'You mean with women my own age?' he asks me.

'No, that's not what I mean at all,' I quickly reply in case he is offended. 'I just think it's such a shame that you have your health, your wealth, and this beautiful apartment, but nobody to share it with. You could have another twenty years of life ahead of you. Don't you want to make the best of it?'

Charles goes quiet for a moment, and I worry I've said too much. Why didn't I just sip my drink and make small talk instead of trying to get all deep? He'll probably tell me to leave now, and the possibility of that makes me keep speaking.

'You're such a nice man. You shouldn't be paying people to be with you. It's a privilege to be in your company.'

Maybe it's all the alcohol talking, but I'm finding myself saying anything I can to make him smile. I know this is the last time I will see him, so I want to make sure I leave him feeling good about himself. I mean every word I say. Charles is a lovely man, but if he isn't careful, then somebody might come along and take advantage of that, and they'll be after a lot more than a few thousand pounds.

'You know what, my dear, I think you might be right,' Charles says, nodding his head. 'It can't do any harm to try. And it doesn't have to mean that I love Mary any less, does it?'

'Of course not,' I tell him, placing my hand on his knee as a show of support. But I quickly remove it when I notice him look down at it.

I take another sip of my drink and decide to just finish it quickly now so I can get going for my train, when I feel Charles put his hand on my own leg.

'I am going to miss you,' he says, though I notice he isn't looking at my face now and rather at my bare legs in my long skirt.

'I'll miss you too,' I say, taking another hearty gulp of my drink, and now it's almost gone.

Charles's hand remains on my leg, however, and the longer it does, the more I start to feel uncomfortable about it.

'I really should be going if I want to catch my train,' I tell him, finishing my drink and placing the glass down on the small table beside the sofa.

'What's the rush? Have another. There's plenty more where that came from,' he says, standing up and making his way back over to his bar.

'No, honestly. I'm fine, thank you,' I say, and I stand up and go to put on my coat.

'I suppose you'll be wanting your money, then,' he says rather despondently, but after the slight shift in atmosphere in this flat over the last minute or so, I'm not even bothered about that. I just want to get going before this gets any more awkward.

'Look. Don't worry about the money. Spend it on somebody you really like. I'll just get going.'

I start putting on my coat, but Charles waves his hand dismissively at me as he finishes his drink.

'No, no. A deal's a deal,' he says, and he places his empty whiskey glass down on the bar before heading for the large floor-to-ceiling cupboard beside the enormous flatscreen TV.

He touches the surface of the cupboard, which unlocks it instantly, and Charles pulls it open to reveal several shelves hidden inside the piece of furniture. There are leatherbound books, several large awards, which I presume are from his theatre days, and even a photo of him with a famous Hollywood A-lister. But it's the item on the middle shelf that catches my eye the most.

He has a safe too.

And it's much bigger than mine.

'Seriously, don't worry about it,' I say, heading for the door as Charles turns his back to me.

'I always pay my debts,' he says, and I see him place his thumb over the keypad on the front of the safe, which results in a loud clicking sound before the door pops open.

That's when I see the tall piles of cash stacked inside.

There must be tens of thousands of pounds in there.

I guess I'm not the only one who doesn't trust the banks.

I watch as he removes a bundle of notes from the safe and counts out what he owes me before he makes his way over to where I stand.

My eyes are on the money as he approaches, but I can tell that his eyes are firmly on me.

'Here you go. Thank you for spending time with me. I hope it wasn't too painful for you,' he says as he hands me the money.

'Charles, don't be like that,' I say as the notes are thrust into my hand. I knew I wasn't going to feel great about taking extra money from him, but I didn't think I would feel this bad. But just before he lets go of the cash into my hand, he pulls it back.

'You know, there's plenty more money to be made if you want it,' he tells me, nodding his head in the direction of the open safe behind him.

My eyes drift to the piles of money over his slouched shoulders.

'All you have to do is make an old man happy,' he says, reaching out and running his hand along the tips of my blonde hair.

I wonder if he knows it is a wig. Would he hate the fact that I'm really a brunette? But I have bigger things to worry about right now.

'I just want to go,' I say, stepping back a little in the direction of the door.

'But I want you to stay,' Charles replies, and he suddenly grabs my wrist to prevent me from moving away any further.

I'm startled not just by the action but the strength he possesses as he holds on to me. He's certainly much stronger than he looks, and suddenly his frail frame doesn't seem quite so fragile anymore.

I pull away, but Charles refuses to loosen his grip, and now I'm really worried.

'What are you doing?' I ask him, and it's impossible to disguise the amount of fear in my voice as I speak.

'I'm giving you what you want,' comes the chilling reply as he pulls me towards him again so that my face is now only inches away from his.

Suddenly there is no sign of the friendly, docile, and grieving man I have been around for the last several weeks in the wine bars, restaurants and theatres of the

West End. Instead, Charles just looks like all of the other men I have known in my life.

Selfish, angry, and desperate.

I try to free my wrist from his grip again, but it's no good. He is stronger than me, even at his age.

'Why are you fighting?' he asks me in a terrifyingly calm tone. 'Just spend the night with me, and I'll give you all the money you need. Isn't that what you want?'

'I don't want it,' I say defiantly, and the fear of what might happen if I don't get out of this situation allows me to summon up enough strength to be able to push the old man away from me.

Charles stumbles backwards, and the money he was holding falls to the floor. But I don't look down at the cash scattered all around my feet now. I'm too busy heading for the door.

But it's locked.

'Open this door!' I cry out, desperately fumbling with the catch and turning the handle.

Then I hear something click. I've managed to unlock it.

But before I can open it and run, I feel Charles's hands on my shoulders, dragging me back into the apartment.

'You're not going anywhere,' he says behind me, and I do my best to hang onto the door handle, but I lose my grip, and now I'm falling backwards onto the carpet.

The two of us land on the pound notes scattered across the floor, and we wrestle as I try to get up while Charles tries to keep me down. In the tussle, he grabs a handful of my hair, and my wig comes clean off, leaving him temporarily surprised but giving me the opportunity to get back to my feet and run for the door again.

I reach it, and I'm just about to swing it open when Charles slams me into it hard, and I hit my head against the frame. Now everything is spinning, and I'm sure I can feel blood running from my nose. But I can also feel his hands on me again, and now I'm too dizzy to make him stop.

He holds me against the door, and I'm not sure if his plan is to drag me away again or just try to rape me right here where we stand, but as my focus returns, I'm able to spot the gold statuette sitting on the table to my left.

I reach out for it, but it's just beyond my grasp. But the sound of Charles's heavy breathing as he forces himself on me gives me the strength I need to lunge to the side and grab it.

As I seize the solid object, the sudden momentum of my body sends me falling to the floor, and I hit the carpet hard. But before I can get back to my feet, Charles is right behind me. A slight groan escapes his lips as he lowers himself to his knees and looks to get on top of me, and I notice the crazy look in his eyes as he prepares to take what he wants.

But before he can, I swing the statuette , striking him in the temple and knocking him onto the floor beside me.

It was obvious from the sickening sound of his skull cracking open that Charles wouldn't get up from that.

I lie on the carpet for a few moments to get my breath back, but it's mainly because I know the danger is over now. Charles is not moving, nor is he making a sound. His body lies still beside me, and I can no longer hear his heavy breathing.

When I do eventually get back to my feet, I notice the blood on several of the notes scattered around the floor. At first, I worry that it has come from me, and I put my hand on my nose, checking the damage after I went head first into the door. But there is no blood. It's not mine.

It's his.

I see the pool of velvet seeping out from behind the old man's head as he lies in front of me with his eyes wide open and his body still.

I don't bother to check if he is still alive. I already know he's dead.

Now I just need to get out of here.

It's only when I return to the door that I remember my wig is still in the apartment. I turn back to retrieve it and find it only a few yards away from where his body lies. But as I pick it up and return it to my head, I see the open safe across the room and the vast treasures that sit within it.

I contemplate what would happen if I just left right now. I might get away with this if I'm lucky. But that would be all. I wouldn't come out of this awful event with anything but a bad memory of the attack.

Unless...

It's an instinctive decision, made in a split second, and it almost feels as if my brain shuts down for a moment while my body goes into action.

I pick up my handbag from where it fell on the floor and rush to the safe before scooping out as much of the cash as I can fit inside. But it's barely big enough to hold more than a couple of stacks of notes, so I enter a bedroom and find a small rucksack underneath the bed. Returning to the safe, I frantically pull out the rest of the money, but in my desperate state of mind, I also take a couple of items of jewellery too, including a watch and a ring. Then I close the safe door, and when I try to open it again, it won't release because I know it needs Charles's prints to open. Hopefully, the police will never know the contents were stolen when they eventually enter this apartment and see the dramatic scene inside.

Zipping the rucksack up, I head for the door, checking as I go that there is nothing left behind that could tie me to what happened here tonight.

My glass.

I rush over to the bar and pick up the one I was drinking from, stuffing that into the bag too. I'll throw it in the river on my way out of here.

As I open the door and step outside, I take one last look back at the scene behind me.

The locked safe. The solitary whiskey glass on the bar. And Charles's body lying on top of the bloodied cash.

Then I close the door behind me and go home.

30

AMANDA

From my position on the carriage floor, the photo of Charles in the newspaper stares back at me beneath the headline:

MYSTERY AROUND MURDERED DIRECTOR REMAINS UNSOLVED ONE MONTH ON

The image in the paper shows him how the world knew him, a suave and friendly gentleman in a suit smiling at the camera. But the image I see in my mind is the one of his true self: the angry, frustrated man with the evil glint in his eye.

It's nice that there is no photo of what he looked like when he died in the article, but that doesn't mean I can stop seeing the image of his bloodied body returning to me whenever I close my eyes. But right now, there's no time for looking back at the past.

I need to get to my feet before I'm caught.

Pushing myself up off the train floor and brushing off the help of a fellow passenger, I scoop up the mobile phone and continue on toward the toilets. A quick glance over my shoulder tells me that my pursuer has suffered an unexpected hold-up of his own, and it's the bit of good luck I have been lacking today. A rotund passenger has stepped out of his seat and into the aisle, effectively blocking the man who is chasing me down and giving me back the precious few seconds I lost when I fell. Now I'm closing in on the toilet door, and thanks to the dithering passenger, I'm certain I'm going to make it in time.

The green light above the toilet door tells me that it is unoccupied, and it's a relief to get inside and slam the door. But I only feel safe when I turn the lock.

He can't get me now.

I lean against the back of the door and take several deep breaths, but my moment of calm is shattered by the sound of heavy banging behind me.

I move away from the door as I hear the calls from outside.

'Open up! Now!'

It's him.

'I'm serious, Amanda! Open this door, or you'll regret it!'

That might be true, but I'll definitely regret it if I do open it, so I stay away from the door and look down at the phone in my hands.

It requires a four-digit access code to open it. But unlike the owner of this phone who is so desperate to know my code, I believe I already have the digits that I need.

I type in the code from memory based on what I watched him typing in every time he unlocked his device during our conversations. It's a little tricky because from where I was sitting, the phone was upside down, but I think I can figure it out.

2846.

The screen unlocks. I'm in. Now I can see the messages from James. But that's not all.

I can also see the photo of my daughter tied up to my bed.

My stomach lurches as I see the look of fear in Louise's eyes, and I get the same feeling of anger welling up inside me that I felt the first time I was shown the photo back at the table. But unlike then, I can actually do something about the situation now. I can try to bring an end to it without Louise getting hurt or without me having to open that safe.

I type out a message and read it through a couple of times to make sure it is okay before I hit send.

"Plan is cancelled. Leave the flat and meet me at the station."

I'm not sure if it's going to work, but I press Send anyway. I'm hoping that James will believe the message to be true and leave my daughter at the flat. Considering the text came from his partner's phone, it shouldn't raise too much suspicion. But I need to know that he has complied with the order and left so I can then call the police. I don't want them turning up when he is still there because if they do, he will know something has gone wrong and he might hurt Louise. But I won't know that unless he replies with confirmation.

I stare at the phone, waiting and hoping to see a message come back from James. As I do, his partner continues to hammer on the toilet door, and I'm starting to worry that he might come through. He must know that I'm never going to open it while he is out there. If I can, I'm going to stay in here all the way to the end of the line now.

Suddenly, the shouting and banging stop, and I can hear low voices talking on the other side of the door.

I'm not sure who he is talking to. Another passenger? A train employee? Security? Somebody must have heard all the noise he was making and come to investigate. Maybe they'll arrest him for causing a disturbance.

That would be a big help to me. As long as I have his phone, he can't tell James to hurt Louise.

But where is James? Why hasn't he replied? Has he even seen my message?

Or am I already too late?

31

JAMES

I think I've managed to stop most of the bleeding after Louise kicked me in the face. I dab the tissue against my nose a couple more times to check, and there are a few splotches of red, but nowhere near as much as ten minutes ago. The bleeding has stopped. But I suspect it will be a while until the pain does.

I toss the tissue into the toilet and flush it away before leaving the bathroom and heading back into the bedroom where my prisoner is currently tied up. My head was spinning after the initial kick, and it took all of my restraint not to hurt Louise in the immediate aftermath, but I kept my cool. I'd rather not have to hurt her. I'd much rather her mother just gives up that code, and I can get out of this flat as soon as possible. But time is running out, and I'm willing to do whatever it takes, and if that means drawing blood from Louise, then so be it, particularly after she just drew blood from me.

I walk back into the bedroom, and I'm just about to take out my phone to see if there are any updates from the train when I freeze.

The bed is empty.

The bedpost is snapped.

Louise has gone.

I look around the room for any sign of her, but I can't see her anywhere. Panicking, I turn back to the door, worrying that she has already left the flat while I was in the bathroom. But I would have heard her leave, and I definitely would have seen her. She couldn't have got to the door without passing the bathroom first.

That's when I hear the creak of the wardrobe door to my left and turn around just in time to see Louise bringing the broken piece of bedpost down at my head.

I raise my hands to protect myself, but I'm too late to stop it striking me across my forearms.

The bedpost cracks against my bone, and I let out a cry of pain as I fall back against the wall.

I see Louise run from the bedroom, and I know exactly where she is going, but I'm not letting her get away from me now. I don't even care about the safe at this moment.

I just want to hurt her.

Giving chase, I quickly catch her up and dive on her before she can make it to the front door. We wrestle on the cold, hard tiles of the kitchen, but I quickly gain the upper hand and have her pinned beneath me, where she continues to try to wriggle free but is unable to escape my grasp.

'Let's see how you like it when I hit back,' I say, and I'm just about to get my revenge on my troublesome prisoner when I feel the vibration in my pocket.

I use one arm to keep Louise pinned beneath me as I take out the phone with my free hand, and that's when I see the message. I was hoping it was the code but no such luck.

"Plan is cancelled. Leave the flat and meet me at the station."

What does he mean the plan is cancelled?

'Get off me!' Louise cries as she continues to writhe beneath me, but I keep my body weight on top of her as I try to figure out what could have caused this message to be sent to my phone.

The only way the plan would possibly be cancelled would be if my partner saw no way for it to be successful. Has something happened on that train? Is Louise's mum a more formidable foe than we thought?

I need to find out before I leave. I can't just take his word for it. We've come this far. I have to know why he wants to give up now. But I can't do that until I deal with the problem of the escaping prisoner.

'Stop it, or I'll hurt you!' I say to the woman beneath me, and I raise my fist to emphasise my point.

But Louise refuses to give in, and she's clearly willing to take a beating as long as she has a chance of escape. My fists aren't enough to threaten her. But the knife I held to her feet earlier clearly was.

I reach out for the drawer above us where I found that first knife and fumble around inside for another one. It's not easy with Louise trying to escape beneath me, but I feel the cold, hard steel of another blade in the drawer and lift it out before holding it above my head so she can get a good look at it.

'No!' Louise cries, and she stops fighting instantly, clearly afraid that she has pushed me too far and I'm about to plunge this knife into her as punishment.

'I meant it when I said I didn't want to hurt you,' I say. 'But I will if you keep fighting!'

Louise's fearful eyes remain on the blade above her head.

'If I get off you, then you have to promise not to try to run again, or I swear to God I will kill you.'

Louise nods her head, and I slowly climb off her and

get to my feet. I keep a firm grip on the handle of the knife as Louise crawls away from me until her back is resting against the kitchen table, where she sits and watches me, cowering in fear at what I might do next.

But for the time being, she is no longer my biggest concern. What I need to do is find out why the plan is cancelled. I haven't put myself through all of this for nothing, and I'm not prepared to walk away from a safe full of money unless there is a damn good reason to.

But I'm not going to waste time sending a text message back to that train and waiting for a response.

Instead, I'm going to call.

32

C*ome on. Text me back. Tell me you have left the flat.* I'm still standing in the train toilet, waiting to get a response from James to say he has left Louise alone before I use this phone to call the police, but so far there is nothing. The radio silence is making me more anxious as my imagination runs wild as to why there has been no response yet.

Has he even seen the message? Is he ignoring it? Is he harming Louise right now?

The shock from the phone suddenly vibrating in my hand almost causes me to drop it, and I look down at the screen to see an incoming call.

It's James.

I panic as I try to figure out the best thing to do. I obviously can't answer it because then he will know it's me and not his partner, but if I ignore it, then what will happen? But if he is calling because he suspects something is wrong, it will only make things worse if there is no answer.

What do I do?

My finger hovers over the screen, and I'm just about

to make my decision when there is a loud knock on the toilet door.

'Hello? Is everything okay in there?'

It's a male voice, but I don't recognise it. It's definitely not the man I'm hiding from. *But where has he gone?*

'I've got your boyfriend out here, and he's worried about you,' the voice says.

My boyfriend? What is he talking about?

Then I figure it out. My pursuer must have explained away all the commotion as an argument between a warring couple. I bet he's making out like he is the concerned boyfriend right now and I'm the troubled girlfriend. But I'm not going to let him talk his way out of this that easily.

'He's not my boyfriend!' I call back.

That should do it, and the silence from the other side of the door suggests so. But I can't relax yet. I look down at the phone and see that it's no longer ringing.

I didn't answer.

What will James think of that?

'Look, I don't want to get involved in any dispute the two of you may be having, but you can't stay in the toilet,' the man calls out again. 'There are other people out here who need to use it.'

I'm guessing this guy works on the train in some capacity. Maybe he's a ticket inspector, or perhaps he's just a guy who sells the crisps at the shop in carriage four. I've never visited that shop because I didn't want to start another bad habit that I wouldn't be able to break on my commute after the whole G & T phase, but I know it's there. Or maybe it's just a passenger who really needs to use the loo. But the last thing I need right now is a busybody sticking his nose in.

Whoever it is, I don't care.

I'm not coming out until we get to Brighton.

'Use another toilet!' I cry, shaking my head and looking back at the phone.

Is James going to call back? I'd rather he sent a text because then at least I would know what he is thinking. Either way, I just need to find out if Louise is okay. Maybe I should have answered the call.

Am I just making things worse?

'Open up now!'

The man outside is clearly not going away. But I'm not budging either, and I decide that the best thing to do is just ignore him. He can't get in until the door gets unlocked in Brighton, and by then I imagine the man I'm trying to evade will be fleeing the train.

The phone vibrates again in my hand, and I look down to see I have received another text.

It's James.

"What's happening?"

I type a quick reply.

"Police officers on the train. I can't risk it. Have you left the flat?"

I hold my breath as I wait for the reply.

"No. Still here. Louise is a problem."

The message sends a shiver of dread down my spine because I don't know what he means by that. But I'm also a little proud of my daughter for not making it easy for her captor—just like I haven't made it easy for mine.

Maybe we're not as different as I thought.

"Forget about her. Just leave her and get out. Text me when you've left."

I press Send again and wait.

There is still some commotion on the other side of the toilet door, but I ignore it and keep my focus on the phone.

A minute goes by without a response, and I'm not

sure if that's a good or bad thing. Maybe James is leaving, which is why he hasn't replied. Or maybe Louise is still causing him problems.

I admire my daughter for obviously putting up a fight at the flat, but I pray she hasn't gone too far. From what I can tell with these men, they need us far more than we need them. If they hurt either of us before they get the code to the safe, they'll never get the money, so I'm confident that Louise won't be in real danger unless she pushes James too far.

But knowing my daughter, I wouldn't put it past her.

Finally, the phone vibrates again. It's another text from James.

"How do I know it's really you?"

Damn it.

"Of course it's me. Stop wasting time. We're almost in Brighton."

I hope my quick reply will do the trick.

But I'm wrong. James is calling me again.

This time I decide to answer the phone, but I make sure to say nothing.

'Is this really you?' James asks.

I can hardly impersonate a man's voice, so I stay quiet, but I feel like my plan is falling apart at the seams with every silent second that goes by, and I get confirmation of that when James speaks again.

'I know this is you, Amanda. Well, guess what? Your daughter is going to pay for this now.'

That's when I hear Louise scream in the background again. At least I know she is still alive. But this has gone too far now. I'm out of options.

'Wait!' I beg. 'I'll do it! I'll give you the code!'

This is it. It's over. I tried my best, but I can't keep the contents of that safe secret forever.

It's time for the truth to come out.

33

ONE MONTH EARLIER

I try to enter the flat as quietly as I can. It's eleven o'clock, and Louise might be in bed now. I'm certainly hoping that she is. I doubt she would have bothered waiting up for me, and I wouldn't blame her. But I'm glad not to see her as I creep through my front door, and I'm hoping I can make it all the way into my bedroom without running into her. That's because I'm currently in possession of the contents from Charles's safe, and the last thing I need is to see another person before I can shove them into my own safe and lock the door.

I'm halfway past the sofa when I hear a sound from my daughter's bedroom. It sounds like the television. She is still awake, but it's no problem as long as she doesn't come out and...

Louise's bedroom door suddenly swings open, and

my daughter spots me just before I can make it to my room.

'What time do you call this?' she asks me, but it's not in a sarcastic tone that would be suitable for a child scolding their parent about staying out late. It's done in her usual argumentative manner, which tells me she is annoyed at the fact I've been out all night.

'Oh, you're still up,' I reply, feigning surprise and doing my best to stay calm. 'I was trying to be quiet. I thought you might be asleep.'

'I've been waiting up to see if you were ever going to come back.'

'Of course I've come back. Don't be silly.'

'Is it silly? You've hardly been here these last few months. You keep leaving me alone with nothing to eat and nothing to do, yet you go mad if I ever dare to stay out late during the week.'

'I know, and I'm sorry. Work's been crazy today. We've got a deadline for the end of the week and—'

I hate lying to my daughter, and it's only now I realise how much I have been doing that lately. Perhaps my daughter isn't the only one to blame for our constant arguments. Maybe I should have been making an effort to be around more.

'I don't care about your stupid deadlines!' Louise says, confirming what I just thought. 'What kind of mother leaves her daughter alone all night without calling to say where she is?'

'I was working. Where else would I be?'

'I don't know. The point is you didn't even call!'

'Because I was working!'

The initial fear I had about being seen entering my flat with my ill-gotten gains has faded a little, and I feel myself growing annoyed at my daughter for her attitude. She has no idea of what I've been through this evening, and while she can never know, I wish she weren't giving me this problem right now.

'Have you actually been working? Or have you been on a date?' Louise asks, and my breath catches in my throat.

'What are you talking about?' I reply, looking down at my clothes nervously in case I have left something on that can give me away. But I haven't. I always make sure to get changed in the toilets on the train on the way home after my escorting work, and tonight was no different.

Though of course, tonight was very different.

'I don't believe you've been working,' Louise says. 'I think you're seeing someone. Are you?'

I'm not sure where she has got this idea from, but I decide that she is just speculating and taking her bad mood out on me.

'I'm not going to argue with you at this time of night,' I reply, heading for my bedroom. 'I'm going to bed.'

'Tell me about your new boyfriend? I can't wait to hear all about this next guy. Is he going to take all of your money like the last one did?'

I grit my teeth as I resist the urge to turn around and have it out with my daughter. She blames me for what happened with Johnny and the money, which is a little harsh even though I could have been more careful, so I'd like nothing more than to give her a piece of my mind right now, but I can't stop. I need to get Charles's things into my safe as quickly as possible.

'Why have you got a rucksack?' she asks me, but I ignore that, which I know is only going to irritate her even more. 'Great, just disappear on me like you always do!' she cries as I enter my bedroom, and I make sure to close the door behind me before I remove the bag from my shoulder.

I hear the sound of my daughter's bedroom door slamming as I go into my wardrobe where my safe is located. Kneeling down on the carpet, I enter the eight-digit code into the keypad and hear the click that lets me know I'm in.

Opening the safe, I see the money already in there, which consists mainly of my hard-earned savings from my dual jobs in purchasing and escorting. There's nearly £20,000 in there already. But there's about to be a whole lot more.

I reach into my handbag and take out the first stacks of cash and stuff them inside the safe as quickly as I can, paranoid that Louise might burst in here to continue the argument and catch me with all this money.

Then I unzip the rucksack and work fast until all the cash is out before searching around at the bottom of the bag for the watch and ring I also took in my haste.

It was a moment of madness to take more than just money, although it's been a night full of such moments. I should just throw them away because I have no idea how I will sell these items. I obviously can't do it legally in case they are traced back to Charles's flat and I'm implicated. The safest thing to do would be to get rid of them. But how much are they worth? Can I really afford to throw money away? I might as well sell them, and a dodgy pawnshop in the East End will be my best bet, but that's a problem for another day.

I locate the watch quickly and toss it on top of the money. But I can't see the ring?

Where is it? Did I drop it on the way?

Another quick search of the rucksack yields no immediate results, so I tip the entire contents of my handbag out onto the carpet beside me to speed it up. I rummage through my possessions. Purse. Mobile phone. Mirror. Lipstick. A work email that I printed off before I left the office and really need to read before the big meeting tomorrow.

And one gold ring.

I pick it up off the carpet, but before I put into the safe, I take a second to have a closer look at it. The gold surface shimmers in the light from the bulb above my head, and I wonder how valuable it could be. Knowing Charles, it certainly won't be cheap. Then I notice something on the inside of the band.

Is that an engraving?

I hold it up to my eye, and the writing is small, but I can just about make it out.

Charles & Mary Montague 23.05.70

The piece of jewellery falls from my hand as I realise what it says. This isn't just any ring. This is Charles's wedding ring.

It's got his damn name on it.

Suddenly, my bedroom door swings open, and Louise bursts in.

'What are you doing?' I cry, but it's not going to stop her seeing what I'm up to. I quickly scoop the ring up and stuff it into my back pocket before standing up and trying to close my wardrobe door before my daughter can see the open safe inside. But it's too late.

'Why are you being all secretive?' she asks me, reaching out to pull the wardrobe door open again.

My safe sits open below us, and even though I kick the door closed with my foot, it's not going to be enough to stop Louise realising I was using it.

'What's really in that safe?' she asks me as I try to shut the wardrobe door again.

'None of your business!' I tell her, even though I know she is going to make it her business to find out now.

'Why are you keeping secrets from me? What's in there?' she asks me, trying to open the wardrobe door, but I make sure she can't do that. The safe is still unlocked, and there's no way I'll be able to explain having so much cash in there if she sees it all. I haven't counted it yet, but I imagine there must be at least fifty or sixty grand to go with the twenty I had already.

There's no way I can pass that off as savings from my office job.

'Louise, stop it!' I beg, and in my desperation to keep my daughter from opening the wardrobe, I end up pushing her back across the room, causing her to fall into my bedside table.

'Oh, my God, I'm so sorry!' I say, rushing to my daughter's aid. 'Are you okay?'

As Louise gets to her feet, I see that she isn't hurt from the fall so much as she was hurt by the fact that I caused it, and she pushes past me out of the bedroom in disgust. I know I should go after her, but my safe is still open, so instead, I just brace myself to hear her bedroom door slam again. That's always the noise that signals the end of one of our arguments, and there it is again, right on cue. But that one was louder than all the previous ones combined.

I want to go in and check on her to make sure she is alright, but then I remember the piece of incriminating evidence is currently still on my person, so I rush back to the wardrobe and open the door.

Taking the ring from the back pocket of my jeans, I put it in the safe before quickly locking it. At least that is one drama dealt with for now. Tomorrow, I will get rid of the ring that could tie me to Charles's murder, but for now, I need to go and check on my daughter.

I also need to tell her what I keep in the safe, otherwise she won't stop asking, and she won't stop trying to catch me using it again. I decide that I'll tell her about the £20,000 I have been saving up from my office job and that I bought the safe because I no longer trust the banks after the incident with Johnny. That much is true, and she can know that.

But I'll hold off on letting her know what else is in there.

That much she can never know.

Nobody can.

34

I grip the phone tightly to my ear as I prepare to reveal my deepest and darkest secret.

I haven't been fighting so hard all this time because of the money. While I hate to lose such a large amount, I wouldn't be risking my daughter's life over that. What I have been fighting for is the other thing in that safe that shouldn't be there.

Charles's ring.

It's the one thing that can tie me to his murder if anybody should find it, and it's still in my safe.

I know I should have just thrown the ring away as soon as I saw the engraving. Then I wouldn't have had so much to worry about now. I was going to. I took it out of the safe the morning after I brought it home, and I planned to throw it into the Thames on my way into the office that day. But then I foolishly went looking online for a valuation on the piece of jewellery, found a photo of a similar one and saw how much it was worth.

Online estimates put it anywhere between £10,000 and £15,000.

How could I throw that much money away?

Instead, I had made another plan. I would have the engraving removed from the ring so I would be able to sell it on without the new owner seeing what was previously written on it. I planned to have that done somewhere local rather than in London, where the news of Charles's death would be more prominent. But I underestimated how much of a big name the dead director was in the performing arts world. The discovery of his body and the mysterious circumstances surrounding it didn't just end up in the newspapers in London. It ended up on the front pages of several national newspapers too, thus making me less confident about having the engraving removed at any high street store in the UK for fear that the engraver would recognise the name.

As the days went by and with the story of Charles's death not showing any signs of disappearing from the daily news bulletins after his daughter discovered his body, the ring stayed in my safe. So then I formed a new plan. I was going to take the Eurostar to Paris after leaving my job at the end of the week, where I would have the engraving removed by a Frenchman with no knowledge of the murder victim's name back in London. Then I would be free to pawn it without risk of attracting the attention of the police, and that would be an extra several thousand pounds to help fund the next stage of my life.

But then today happened.

For the last month, my safe has stayed locked, which means I have been in control of the secret it contains. But as soon as it is opened by somebody else, then all that control is lost. I will have no power over what happens next. I could take losing all that money, as painful as it might be considering what I went through to end up with it, but not the risk of being found to be the one behind Charles's brutal murder. I wouldn't just lose my savings then.

I'd lose my freedom, and Louise would be alone with no income, no home and the shame that comes with everybody knowing what her mother had done.

But what if James gets caught with it? What if the police find out what these two men have done and trace back their crimes to me? If they know the ring came from my safe, they will know I was the one who was in Charles's flat that night.

But what other choice do I have? A quick check on my watch tells me that we aren't far from arriving into Brighton, and if I haven't given up the code by then, Louise will pay for my silence. I'm just going to have to bite the bullet and hope for the best. I've tried to put it off as long as I can.

'I'll give you the code if you promise to let my daughter go,' I say into the phone.

'No. Code first, then I'll let her go,' James replies.

'At least let me speak to her so I know she is all right,' I try.

'I don't have time for this! Give me the code!'

'Let me speak to my daughter first!'

I'm determined not to give in until he does as I ask, reminding myself that he has nothing without the information I can give him.

'Fine. You've got ten seconds,' he replies, and the line goes quiet for a moment.

'Mum?'

It's great to hear my daughter's voice, even if she does sound absolutely terrified.

'Lou, are you okay? I'm so sorry about this.'

'Just come home, Mum. Please.'

'I'm on my way right now, and I'll be there soon. Are you hurt?'

'No, I'm fine,' Louise replies, and the sound of her meek voice tells me that she is anything but.

'Are you tied up?'

'No.'

'Okay, I need you to listen to me. I'm going to give him the code to the safe. But I need you to do something while he is opening it. I need you to try to get away from him. Run and lock yourself in the bathroom while his back is turned. Do you think you can do that?'

The line goes quiet.

'Louise?' I cry, terrified at what the silence means.

'Ten seconds is up,' James says. 'Give me that code.'

I take a deep breath.

'Okay. The code is 87219923.'

I slump down onto the closed toilet seat as I keep the phone to my ear. I'm exhausted and angry, but I just want this to be over with now.

Gripping the device tightly, I wait for James to talk to me again or hang up. I won't know which until he reaches the safe. As I wait, I can hear more talking on the other side of the toilet door, but I still can't hear the man who chased me in here. I wonder if he has given up now and moved to a different part of the train, perhaps preparing to get off quickly when the train reaches the station, and disappear before I can point him out to the police in Brighton. He probably presumes I've already called 999 from in here and that they are on the way to the flat, as well as the train station. But I haven't. I've given his partner what he wants.

'Give me that code again?' James asks, bringing the temporary silence on the phone to an end.

'87219923,' I repeat, keeping my voice calm.

I can hear the sound of the keys being pressed on the safe, and it gives me severe anxiety to know that somebody other than me is pressing them, but there's not much I can do about it from here.

'It's not working,' James repeats.

'What? Are you sure you're putting it in right?'

I wonder if Louise has had a chance to run into the bathroom yet while James is distracted. He hasn't shouted after her yet, but then he is preoccupied with getting his hands on a bundle of money. But then James speaks again, and I suddenly feel like the walls of the train toilet are closing in on me.

'I'm not the one entering it. It's your daughter.'

Shit.

James has got Louise doing it for him.

I was expecting him to do it.

I was hoping he would be distracted while he was at the safe, giving her a chance to run and hide. But she is the one pressing the keys on the safe. That means I have just put her in even more danger.

'It's been temporarily locked for ten minutes! What the hell have you just done?' James cries down the phone, aware now that something is wrong.

My safe comes with a feature that means it won't open for ten minutes if the incorrect code has been entered three times in a row. I knew that would happen because I had given him the wrong code, but that was only because I thought Louise would be safely locked in the bathroom by now.

Instead, the sound of her screams down the phone tell me that James is finally making good on his threat of hurting her.

Oh, my God, I've killed my daughter.

35

AMANDA

'No! Stop! I'm sorry! I got the numbers mixed up! I'll give you the right code! Just don't hurt her! Please!'

I'm a terrible mother for risking my daughter's life, but I thought there was one last genuine chance to get out of this without letting him in that safe. If Louise could have made it to the bathroom and locked the door while James was distracted, then she would have been safe when he discovered that the code was wrong. Then James would have had no choice but to give up and leave before I called the police, and disaster would have been averted. The ring would still be locked away, and my secret would still be safe. But I've messed it all up now, and it sounds like James has never been angrier.

'You stupid bitch!' he yells at me through the phone, and I'm not sure what he's doing to Louise, but she sounds in pain.

'I'm sorry! I'll give you the code! Please leave her alone!' I beg.

Then the line goes dead.

'No!' I scream, jumping up from the toilet seat and

checking the phone. But it just confirms what I feared. James hung up on me, and now I have no idea what is happening in that flat.

I desperately hit the button on the phone's screen to call him back, and I pray that he will pick up, but several rings later I have no luck. 'Answer the phone!' I cry out, tears welling in my eyes.

I'll never forgive myself for this. I'm responsible for my daughter's death. I should have just given them what they wanted an hour ago, no matter what I was trying to hide. But it seems like it's too late now.

I call James three more times, but there is still no answer, and every second that ticks by means there is a greater chance that Louise is paying the price for my reckless actions.

If only I could speak to him. If only there was some way to make him stop.

Then I have an idea.

I quickly unlock the toilet door and pull it open, bursting back out into the carriage and hoping to see his partner standing outside, waiting for me.

But he's not here.

No one is.

'No! Where are you?' I call out, looking both ways frantically down the train for any sign of the man. But he's gone.

I make a decision and turn left, heading back in the direction of the table where we were sitting. Maybe he has gone back there. Hopefully, I'll find him sitting in his original seat, and I can get him to send James a message and stop him from whatever he is doing right now. I'll tell him how sorry I am, and I will give them the real code.

No more games.

I try calling James again as I keep moving past the

rows of seats, but there's still no answer, and every second that goes by is making me feel sick with dread.

How will I be able to live with myself if Louise gets hurt?

I reach the carriage where the man and I sat for the majority of this journey, and I hold my breath as I look towards our table at the other end.

Is he there?

No. *The seats are empty.*

I make it back to the table as if to double-check, but the fact it is unoccupied was already clear.

'No, no, no! Where are you?' I say to myself, attracting a few strange glances from the sparsely seated passengers around me. 'The man who was sitting here. Have you seen him?' I ask them, the desperation clear in my voice.

A couple of them shake their heads, but most of them just bury their faces back in their mobiles, and I'm left standing in the aisle, devastated and afraid.

I look down at the phone and think about trying James's number again, but I fear that too much time has already passed. Instead, I slump down into my old seat and hold my head in my hands, and it's not long until the tears start to flow.

I've never been a crier, not even after all the bad things that have happened to me over the years, but none of them compare to what might have just happened now.

I may have just lost the only person in the world I really care about.

'What's the matter, Amanda?'

The recognisable voice sends a shiver down my spine, and I spin around to see its owner standing over me with a grin on his face.

'I believe you have something of mine,' he says, reaching down and snatching his phone from my hand.

I have no idea where he just came from, but I'm relieved to see him.

'You have to get through to James! Make him stop!' I cry. But he's in no rush to do as I ask. In fact, he seems to be revelling in my distress as he slowly retakes his seat opposite me and looks down at his phone.

'I see you two have been chatting,' he says as he scrolls through his phone log. 'What's the matter? Things not go to plan? Isn't it annoying when that happens?'

'You have to get through to him! He's going to hurt her!'

'Of course he is. You haven't done what we asked. You knew the rules, Amanda.'

'We're not at the end of the line yet!' I protest. 'You said I had until the end of the line!'

'That was before you stole my phone and locked yourself in the toilet,' he replies. 'And that was also before you tried to impersonate me to call the whole thing off.'

He turns his phone around to show me that he has found the message I sent to James where I pretended to be him, and he shakes his head at my petulance.

'You broke the rules, Amanda, so you can't be mad if James does the same.'

'Please! You need to speak to him! Tell him to stop!'

'And why would I do that?' he asks me.

'Because I'll give you the code,' I reply, swallowing hard.

He studies me, obviously suspicious, but I hold my hands up as a way of letting him know that I'm done playing games.

'Type it in here,' he says, handing me his phone, and I do as he says, pressing the correct eight numbers that will unlock my safe and expose my secrets and lies to their new owner.

I hand the phone back to him and watch as he writes out a message before he presses send and puts his phone in the inside pocket of his suit jacket.

'I've sent it. But at this point, I can't guarantee that James will even see it, let alone act on it. That's your fault, Amanda, not mine.'

I say nothing.

Instead, I just stare at the horizon through the train window. It's a pretty sunset on the south coast, and the sky has a reddish glow to it. But it's not much consolation, and if anything, the colour only makes me think of bad things.

Danger.

Warning.

Blood.

36

LOUISE

I'm sitting with my back to the wall in the corner of my mum's bedroom, as far away as I can from the dangerous man who I thought was going to kill me a moment ago. James went into a wild rage after the code Mum gave him over the phone failed to work, and as he grabbed me by the hair and dragged me away from the safe, I was convinced that it was over and I was certain to die. The look in his eyes told me that he had lost all control, and I prepared myself for the worst.

It was strange after all the fighting I have done today, but as he loomed over me with that crazed expression on his face, I felt a sense of calm at what was about to happen. I guess they call it giving up. Maybe if Mum and I had given up sooner, then things might have worked out better. But we are both as stubborn as each other, and now it seems that the two of us fought to the bitter end.

But James didn't kill me. Instead, he allowed me to crawl into this corner while he turned back to the safe and kicked it several times. He's angry because the code he told me to input was incorrect, so after three attempts, it ended up deactivating the safe for ten minutes until he could try again. He's been waiting for that time to pass so he can have another go, but I'm not sure what he's hoping to achieve. It's impossible to guess that code. I should know because I have tried to guess it enough times myself ever since I found out the safe existed.

I hoped to break into it and see how much money Mum really had stashed away in there and maybe even take a chunk of it myself. After all, she couldn't stop me going travelling if she came home to find out I'd already gone, could she? But it was no good. I tried as many different combinations as I could while she was at work, and none of them opened it. Birthdays. Anniversaries. Common sequences I found online. None of the eight digits I pressed released the lock and gave me access. But good luck to James. He's experiencing that same feeling of failure right now.

I hear the two beeps that signal when the ten-minute auto lock has expired and watch James as he types in another code only to be unsuccessful again. While I don't feel bad for him, I know what it feels like to be frustrated. He obviously had a plan for how his life was going to work out, and it's gone wrong. Welcome to the club. At least I'm not alone in being utterly miserable.

'Fuck this!' James cries, standing up and giving the safe one last kick before checking the time and shaking his head.

He looks at me sitting in the corner, and I wonder what he is going to do now, but in the end, he just walks out of the room.

Is he leaving?

I daren't move just in case he comes back, but maybe this is finally over. Then I hear the sound of the front door opening, and I guess this is it. He's given up. He's walking out of the flat.

I'm safe!

The door slams shut, and I slowly exhale, but I can't relax for too long. I need to find my phone and call the police. Maybe they can catch James before he gets too far. After what that psycho has put me through, he deserves to be punished.

I get to my feet and head for the bedroom door, praying that James hasn't taken my phone and that it will be lying somewhere in the flat. But as I reach the doorway, I freeze.

James is walking back into the room.

'What are you doing?' I ask him, immediately stepping back and retreating to the corner again. But James ignores me and instead returns to the safe, where he consults his mobile phone before entering yet another combination of digits.

I expect his latest attempt to be just as futile as his previous ones.

But I'm wrong. I hear the lock releasing, and the safe door pops open.

He's in.

'Yes!' James cries, and he turns to me with a smile on his face that I know is supposed to tell me that he has won.

I guess my mum finally gave up the code. Did she do it to save me? Or did she do it to save herself? I don't know. It doesn't really matter. The safe is open now, and everything in there is going to be gone in a minute's time.

'Holy shit!' James cries, and at first, I'm not sure why, until he starts pulling out all the money.

Why is there so much of it?

'Your mum has been saving hard!' he says to me,

shaking his head. 'There must be over fifty grand here. Maybe more!'

I watch as he stuffs the money into his rucksack, and I'm just as shocked as he is at the amount of money in there.

Is this why Mum took so long to give up the code? Is this why she was risking my life?

Where the hell did she get all this money?

James takes out a watch from the safe and examines it before tossing it into his bag as well. I don't recognise that item of jewellery, nor do I recognise what seems to be a gold ring that comes out after it. James shrugs and stuffs the ring into his pocket before double-checking the safe is empty, then stands up and slings his bulky rucksack over his shoulder.

'Well, I have to say this has been worth it,' James says, smiling as he feels the weight in his bag. 'Your mother is a bit of a badass. But she's not the only one.'

He winks at me, and I guess this is what it looks like to be a winner. I spent my whole life trying to get my mum to give me some of her money, and this guy got it all in less than an hour. That would sting if I wasn't already feeling bad enough.

'I guess I'll be going, then,' James says, taking one last look around the room. 'But before I do…'

He reaches back into his bag again, and I dread to think what it is that he might pull out of there. In the end, it's almost a relief to see that it is just more cable ties.

Stepping towards me and grabbing my left wrist, I fight only a little as he secures me to the radiator. I'm done struggling now. I just want him to be gone.

'That should hold you a little longer than the bedpost,' he says with a smirk, making one final check on the strength of the tie before heading for the door.

'Don't bother trying to call the police. You'll need your phone for that,' he tells me, tapping his rucksack to let me know that my mobile is in there too. Then he heads for the door.

'Wait!' I call after him, and he pauses.

'Is my mum okay?'

He takes a moment to think about it before shrugging his shoulders. 'I'm sure she's fine,' he replies. 'My partner isn't as dangerous as me.'

Then he walks away, leaving me alone in the flat.

37

I close the door to the flat behind me and head for the staircase, checking the time on my phone as I go. It's 18:50. The train will be due in any minute. I'll be expected to go straight to the rendezvous point and wait there. But I'm not going to do that because that would result in me sharing what I have in this rucksack, and that was never part of my plan going into today.

Instead, I'm going to take it all for myself.

I make it to the bottom of the staircase before sending a text confirming that I was able to access the safe and that I am on the way now. Then I leave the flats and step out onto the street, trying to keep myself calm despite now being in possession of a life-changing sum of money.

I was told that there was around £20,000 in that safe, and I would have classed that as a good day's work if I'd been able to get it all. But then I opened the door and saw that there was so much more than that. I haven't had time to count it all out yet, but I estimate there could be at least three times that amount just in pure cash now lying in the bottom of my bag. Not only that, but there was what looked to be an expensive watch too, as well as a gold ring, so depending on their value, I could be looking at the best part of £100K.

I haven't done too bad for a guy who got out of prison a month ago.

I hurry down the street, lugging my heavy rucksack as I go, but the heavier the better in this case. I'm tempted to call a taxi to take me to the station, but I know it would be wiser not to. The police will probably be called to the flat when Amanda gets home, and then they'll be interested in knowing if any young males were spotted with a black rucksack in this area around this time. The last thing I need is some taxi driver telling the police that he dropped me off at the station—then they might be able to catch up with me before I leave the country. I'll just make the ten-minute walk to the station instead. I can still make the two trains I need to take tonight even after this delay. That should also give enough time for my partner to leave the station and make his way to the pub on the seafront where we are due to meet up for a debrief.

The pub in question is called the Mermaid and Anchor, and it's where we met to go over this plan way back at the beginning, so it only felt right for it to be the location where we would meet to toast the success of it upon completion. But I won't be showing up at that pub.

I'll be long gone by then.

I feel my phone vibrate in my pocket and take it out as I turn onto the next street. It's another message from my partner on the train.

"Just arriving at the station. See you soon."

I smirk at the words as I put my phone away again. He has no idea what I am about to do to him. But I'm not going to feel bad for double-crossing him. After all, I was the one who met Louise and found out about the safe in the first place. He might have helped me come up with the idea of how to get the money out of it, but without me, there would have been no plan to make. So why should I share this loot with him? He thinks he's so clever with his sharp suits and his sales patter, but I know he is no different from me. He's just a guy trying to get ahead, and I'm confident he would have screwed me over at the first opportunity. But now I'm the one getting ahead, and he's the one who has been screwed.

That will serve him right for cheating in all those poker games we played.

I cross the street and keep my head down as I pass a dog walker on the pavement before turning the next corner and seeing the train station come into view up ahead. I check the time again on my phone, and as I do, I feel the ring in my pocket beside my device.

Taking it out, I have a closer look at it as I continue to the station. It certainly looks like it could be worth a few quid, but I guess I won't know until I take it into a pawnshop and see what I can get for it. Then I notice the small engraving on the underside of the ring, and I pause for a second to read it.

Charles & Mary Montague 23.05.70

I have no idea who they are. Amanda's parents, perhaps. Maybe this is a family heirloom. The thought of that makes me even more excited about the prospect of it being valuable.

I put the ring back into my pocket and focus on the task at hand, which is getting onto my train without being seen by my partner at the station. I'm cutting it close by catching a train at a similar time to when his arrives in, and I hadn't expected it to be as fine as this, but I should still be okay. I had expected Amanda to give up the code much earlier than she did, and then I could have been making my escape while my partner was still miles from Brighton. He never could have caught me then. But I can still make it.

In ten minutes, I'll be sitting on a train to London while he is on his way to that pub on the seafront. But by the time he realises that I've betrayed him, I'll be long gone.

38

I tuck my mobile phone back into the inside pocket of my suit jacket and brush a little speck of dust off the shoulder. I'm feeling slick right now, and it's not just because of my attire. It's taken longer than anticipated, but finally the safe is open and we have the money. As the train makes its arrival into Brighton, I feel like toasting to a job well done, and I won't have to wait long. I'll be meeting James in less than half an hour in a pub on the seafront for a celebratory pint, and together we'll watch the sun go down on the south coast before I take the money for myself and leave him high and dry.

While the mood is high on my side of the table, it's distinctly low on the other. Amanda is leaning on the table with her head in her hands, looking well beaten, which of course she is. She proved a slightly more formidable opponent than I anticipated, and I respect her for that, but in the end, she was no match for me.

'Don't worry. Your daughter is fine, and you can always make more money,' I tell her, deciding not to revel in my win too much and instead show a little respect to my fallen foe. 'By the sounds of it, you have many talents, so I'm sure you won't be short of work.'

Amanda doesn't look up at me, which is a shame because I almost miss that glare of hers. It was quite endearing, in a way.

I feel the brakes engaging on the train and look out of the window to see the edge of the platform at Brighton Station come into view.

Here we are.

The end of the line.

I get up from my seat and brush out the creases in my suit, finding that I'm actually starting to enjoy wearing it now after a little early scepticism. Perhaps I'll use some of my earnings today on a couple of new outfits. Being a wealthy con man certainly beats being a broke one.

'I just want you to know this wasn't personal,' I say to Amanda as I stand in the aisle and look down at the broken woman. 'You've got a good spirit in you. Don't lose that. And good luck with your book.'

As my parting gift, I take out Amanda's mobile from my jacket pocket and place it down on the table in front of her. I don't need to take it.

I've taken more than enough from her today.

With the goodbyes over, I turn and make my way down the carriage as the train comes to a stop, and when the doors slide open, it feels good to step out into the fresh air of a warm summer's evening. But I don't linger too long on the platform, aware that Amanda could still cause me problems right now if she were to raise the alarm with any of the staff at this station. I doubt she will because I can still see her sitting at her table with her phone to her ear as I make my way past the window of the train along the platform, but there's no point hanging around and inviting trouble.

I make my way through the ticket barrier and exit the station, joining the plucky commuters who make this journey from London to Brighton every single weekday evening after a day's work. But while they are now heading for the streets that surround this station for a brief reprieve before coming back in the morning to do the exact same thing again, I am looking forward to tomorrow being a special day. That's because by this time in twenty-four hours, I'll be watching the sun set over the Mediterranean, having swapped the south coast of England for that of France. The plan is for James and me to take the 8 a.m. Eurostar to Paris from London in the morning and head deeper into Europe from there. But I am planning on taking the money and giving him the slip as soon as we are out of the country before heading south to Nice. There I will enjoy the fruits of my labour for as long as the money will last me. With all the fun I'm planning on having with it down on the Riviera, it probably won't last long.

It's always been part of my plan to lose James and claim all the money for myself. I don't owe him anything. I'm the brains who has put this whole operation together, whereas he just got lucky by falling into bed with a young woman whose mum had a bit of cash saved away. Anybody could have done what he did, but very few people could have concocted the scheme that I have come up with, which is why I feel no guilt about betraying my partner.

I nod at the taxi driver standing beside his car on the rank, and he immediately takes the hint and gets in behind the wheel of his vehicle.

'The Mermaid and Anchor, please,' I tell him as I

take my seat in the back of the cab and pull the door closed behind me.

As the car pulls out of the train station car park, I take my phone from my jacket pocket to let James know I will be with him shortly. I expect he is there already. He may even be on his second pint by now. But I wouldn't begrudge him starting without me. He's earned that drink just as much as I have. From the messages he was sending me while I was on that train, it sounded as if Louise was just as much of a nuisance as Amanda was as we went about our work. But just like her mother, she wasn't enough to stop us getting what we wanted.

'Nice night for a pint,' the taxi driver says as he drives me along the Promenade towards the pub.

'You're right,' I reply, smiling as I look out over the pebble beach and the calm blue waters that make this town so popular with tourists. 'It certainly is.'

39

AMANDA

There was no answer from Louise's mobile as I sat in my seat and watched that man walk into the crowd after we arrived at the station, but I wanted to make sure he was gone before I made my own way out. I don't care about catching him. I just want to get back to the flat and see my daughter. The fact she isn't picking up her phone is a cause for concern, and now the man has gone, it's time for me to get back to the flat as quickly as I can.

The taxi driver responsible for getting me back home on this last leg of my journey obviously took the hint that I wasn't in the mood for conversation when I entered his cab, because he hasn't said a single word to me since we set off. It's only a short journey, and I usually walk it, but I don't have the luxury of taking my time tonight, nor do I have the patience to listen to the driver tell me about how busy he has been today. I just thrust a five-pound note into his hand, told him my address, and ordered him to get me home as quickly as he could.

He probably thinks I've had a bad day at the office

and if only that were the truth. I remember so many nights coming home from work feeling fed up, frustrated, and even angry with what I had been through in my job, but those times almost seem like the glory days when I look back on them. The sorrow I felt back then certainly pales in comparison to how I feel after today. I've not only lost everything I have worked for, and everything I gained after being assaulted in Charles's apartment, but that ring is out in the world again, and I have no idea what is going to happen with it. Will the men who have stolen it figure out that it is connected to a murder? Will the police catch them, find the ring, and learn that it was my safe that it was stolen from? Will I ultimately end up losing a lot more than just my savings?

In the end, I'm glad this is only a short journey in the taxi because, otherwise, I feel as if my head would explode with all the terrifying possibilities. Instead, the car is already pulling up outside my flat, meaning I now have something else to distract me.

I need to go inside and see if my daughter is safe.

I slam the car door behind me as I run up the path towards the entrance, my heart already racing long before my legs were. Tapping my electronic key fob onto the access panel, I pull the heavy glass doors open and rush to the staircase, taking the steps two at a time on my way up to the third floor.

Once there, I reach my front door and jam the key into the lock, turning it quickly and bursting inside, afraid at what I might find waiting for me on the other side but desperate to see at the same time. Will Louise come running towards me in relief, or will she be lying dead on the carpet with blood running across her lifeless face?

In the end, neither of those outcomes materialise,

and I see no sign of my daughter as I step inside and close the door behind me.

'Louise! Are you okay?' I yell into my silent home, the stress of the situation threatening to overwhelm me at any moment.

But there's no response. *Oh, my God, they lied to me.* They must have hurt her even with the code. But how badly?

'Mum?'

The sound of her voice from behind my bedroom door is a welcome one, and I rush into the room to see Louise tied to the radiator, looking exhausted but alive.

'You're okay!' I cry as I run towards her and wrap my arms around her slender frame.

'Get me out of this,' she tells me, pulling at her restraint, and I waste no time in rushing into the kitchen before returning with the scissors and cutting through the cable tie.

As she gets to her feet, I move in for another hug, and she doesn't move or say a word as I squeeze her tightly. I'm just so glad to find her alive and well that her silence doesn't even bother me for a minute. But then I eventually let her go, and only then do I notice the look in her eyes.

She isn't scared. She isn't afraid.

She is angry.

'I'm so sorry, Lou. What did he do to you?' I ask, reaching out to take my daughter's hand, but this time she pulls away from me, and when she speaks, it's not to say what I expected her to.

'What did *you* do?' she asks me, turning the question back around.

'What?'

'Why was there so much money in the safe? And jewellery too? Where did all that stuff come from?'

I realise that my daughter must have witnessed James emptying it out and is now well aware that there was a lot more than just £20,000 in there. But before I answer her, I turn and look towards the safe because I need to see it for myself. Even though I know it is empty, I have to confirm it.

Sure enough, the door is open, and there is nothing inside. But I don't get to look at it for long because Louise grabs my arm and spins me around to face her. She wants answers, and she is entitled to them. I just have to figure out which ones I can give her and which ones I must still try to keep a secret.

'Answer me,' Louise begs, her voice cracking with the strain of what she has been through today.

'I haven't been honest with you,' I confess, and despite everything that has happened today, this might be the moment when I feel the worst. The moment when I admit I have been lying to the only person in the world whom I love.

'No shit!' Louise replies. 'Where did all that money come from? Did you rob those guys? Is that why they came after us?'

'No, of course not.'

'Then what did you do, because you sure as hell didn't make that money working in an office.'

'I've been working as an escort!'

There, I've said it. Maybe I should have said it sooner, but it's out there now.

'A what?'

'An escort. Men paid me to go on dates with them.'

Louise looks like she doesn't know whether to laugh or cry.

'An escort? Like a prostitute?' she asks with an expression of disbelief on her face.

'No, of course not!'

'Then what?'

'We just went for dinner and drinks. Sometimes to the theatre. But that's it. There was never anything sexual, I swear.'

'Yeah, right. I saw all that money!' she cries loudly, letting me know that she is going to need more convincing than that.

'That's all from the dates. I swear.'

'It doesn't make sense. Why would guys pay you so much just to go on a date?'

'Because they're lonely. Desperate. I don't know. But I promise nothing physical happened with any of them. I never went back to any of their homes.'

Oh, how I wish that were true.

'I don't believe you,' Louise replies, and it hurts me to see that she means it.

'I'm telling you the truth,' I insist. 'They were just dates. I needed the extra money.'

'And you told me you couldn't give me any money to go travelling.' Louise shakes her head in disgust. 'Yet you had all that cash in there the whole time.'

'Lou, please. I don't want to argue. I'm just glad you're okay.'

'Yeah, I'm fine. I've just found out my mum is a liar and my boyfriend was only with me because he was planning to steal from us!'

Louise turns to storm out of the room, but I reach after her, unable to leave it like this.

'Did he hurt you? Tell me what happened,' I beg her, grabbing her arm and pulling her back.

'Get off me!' she cries, trying to fight against my grip, but I don't let go. This is quickly turning into the worst argument we have ever had until suddenly Louise's anger morphs into something else.

She begins to cry, and now I can see that it was all a

front. She is scared and she is traumatised after what she went through. She was just trying to hide it with another argument. But now the walls have come down, and she is sobbing uncontrollably, which makes me feel dreadful because I know I'm the one who has brought this on my daughter.

'Come here,' I say as I pull her into me, and she buries her face in my shoulder as I hold onto her.

'You're safe now,' I tell her as she weeps, and it breaks my heart to see my daughter like this. I haven't seen her cry since she was a little girl.

It's several seconds until Louise lifts her head from my shoulder and wipes her tear-stained eyes, and I guide her to the edge of the bed, where we take a seat beside each other. But I decide to let her be the one who speaks first for fear of pushing her away again.

'We need to call the police,' she says when she finally gets herself back under control. 'They might be able to catch them.'

'They'll be long gone,' I tell her, even though I know she is right.

'You can't just let them get away with it! They took everything! I thought he was going to kill me!'

I take Louise's hand again before she can get too worked up. 'I'm so sorry. But we can't call the police.'

'Why not?'

I take a moment to pick my answer carefully. 'Because I don't want them knowing about all that money,' I say. 'I hadn't declared it. I can't tell them how much was in there because they will know what I was doing.'

'Who cares? So you weren't paying taxes. I think robbery and attempted murder are slightly worse crimes to commit!'

'It wasn't attempted murder,' I say before instantly

regretting it, and Louise pulls her hand away from mine and gets up from the bed.

'You weren't the one tied to the bed while a guy threatened you with a knife!' she cries.

'You're right. I'm sorry. I didn't mean that,' I try, but it's too late. I've gone and said the wrong thing, and now my daughter is mad at me again.

'What are you hiding?' Louise asks me as she keeps her distance from me when I try to get her to sit down again.

'I'm not hiding anything,' I try. But she isn't buying it.

'Escorting would explain the money. But what about the other stuff that was in there. The watch. The ring. Where did that stuff come from?'

I think about trying to lie my way out of this one too, but I stop when I see how hurt my daughter is. After everything she has been through today, she doesn't deserve that. Maybe I'll regret telling her, and maybe I'll get punished for it, but perhaps that's what I deserve.

'Sit down and I'll tell you,' I say, my voice low and my mood even lower.

Louise does as I ask, and I can feel my heart hammering in my chest as I prepare to reveal my deepest and darkest secret.

'I was telling the truth when I said I didn't go back to the homes of any of my dates,' I begin. 'But there was one exception.'

I take a deep breath before continuing. 'There was one man who asked me to go back, and I did,' I say, and Louise shakes her head at me. 'But it's not what you think,' I quickly add. 'It wasn't for sex. He was much older than me. His wife had passed away, and he was all alone. He had become quite fond of me during our dates and took it badly when I told him that I was going to leave the escorting agency. So he offered me money to come back for one more drink.'

'And you accepted it?'

'It was a lot of money, and he was a lonely old man. I felt sorry for him.'

'What happened?'

My brain is screaming at me to stop talking, but Louise should know the truth, so I press on. 'At first, everything was fine. We had our drink, and he was a gentleman like always. Then I was preparing to leave. That's when he changed.'

'What do you mean?'

'He made a pass at me. I was shocked, not just because of the age difference between us but because he had never even hinted at wanting anything like that from me in all our previous dates.'

'What did you do?' Louise asks, and I can tell that she is afraid of my answer. By now she must have guessed that the jewellery belongs to this man, but I bet she'd never guess how I ended up getting it.

'I tried to leave. He wouldn't let me. He forced himself on me, and he was much stronger than I thought he would be.'

Just reliving that night in my mind is bringing back that terrible feeling when he had me pressed against the door in his apartment. That feeling of not being able to stop what was about to happen. I wouldn't wish it on my worst enemy.

'Oh, my God,' Louise says, and this time she is the one to take my hand.

'We fought. I hit him over the head. He didn't get back up.'

The vivid nature of the memory in my mind means I can almost see his body lying in front of me right now.

'Did you kill him?' Louise asks.

I nod my response.

My daughter doesn't say anything for a few seconds until my anxiety levels reach breaking point and I have to end the silence.

'He was going to rape me. I had to do something. But I never meant to kill him. You have to believe me.'

'Of course I believe you,' Louise says, and it's a relief to have her trust, even if it is over something as bad as this. 'So what happened then?'

'I was going to leave, but then I saw his safe across the room, just sitting there, wide open. It was full of money. I know I shouldn't have, but I guess it was the adrenaline or the shock after what had just happened that made me do it.'

'You took everything?'

I nod my head, feeling almost as ashamed about that as I do about the fact that I killed a man.

'So the watch and ring were his,' Louise says, piecing it all together. 'That's why you don't want to call the police. If they catch them and find out where they got them from, they'll know you killed him.'

I say nothing because there isn't anything else that I can add that will make this situation any better.

'So what do we do?' Louise asks me.

'I don't know,' I reply, and I don't even need to think about lying for that one. 'Maybe I can talk to my manager and ask him to redact my resignation. Or I can find another job. We'll be okay.'

But Louise doesn't say anything. I'm not sure if it's because she is mad at me again or whether she has finally run out of questions to ask. It doesn't matter. I've told her everything there is to know about this sorry situation now.

'I'll call my manager now and see what I can do about my job,' I say, taking out my mobile phone and doing my best to stop the tears welling up in my eyes. I can't believe I'm going to have to beg for a job I couldn't wait to leave. I'm just about to locate his number on my phone when Louise suddenly sits forward.

'Oh, my God. I think I might know a way of finding them!' she says, leaping up from the bed and rushing into her room.

'What?' I call after her, but she doesn't answer me until she returns with her laptop, which she quickly opens and logs onto.

'My phone has that thing where you can check the location on it if you lose it,' she tells me, shaking her head. 'I can't believe I didn't think of it straight away.'

'What does that mean?' I ask her, still not quite caught up with her thought process.

'James took my mobile! It means that as long as he still has it on him, we can see exactly where he is,' she says, typing furiously on her keyboard.

'Really?' I ask, thinking that sounds too good to be true.

'Got it!' she cries, spinning her laptop around to show me the screen. Then she points at it so I can understand what I'm looking at.

'I've just entered my number in here,' she says. 'And this is my phone.'

'That's James?' I ask, watching the flashing red dot.

'Yes!' she replies enthusiastically. 'As long as he holds on to my phone, then we can track him!'

This sounds too good to be true, but I don't doubt what my daughter is telling me.

I see the map.

I see the flashing red dot moving across it.

And I see exactly where the man who stole my money is going.

40

STRANGER

The beer isn't going down as well as I thought it would. I've never been a fan of drinking alone, but I don't have much choice right now.

That's because James isn't here.

I check the time again and see that another ten minutes have passed since I walked into this pub and expected to find him sitting at one of the tables. I was surprised to beat him here and sent him a quick message for an update as I ordered two pints and carried them over to this table in the corner. But there has been no response, nor was there one when I called him a few minutes ago.

Now I'm starting to get worried.

I take another thirsty gulp of my frothy lager and try to quieten the gnawing sense of dread in the pit of my stomach that is telling me that James isn't going to show. Of course he will show. This was the plan. Meet here. Debrief. Check in to the hotel around the corner. Head to London in the morning for the Eurostar. Enter France.

There's no reason to think he has strayed from that schedule.

No reason other than the empty seat across the table from me.

With the alcohol not working on calming my nerves as well as I need it to, I pick up my phone and try James again. One ring. Two. Three. Four. I hang up after six, and now I'm even more anxious.

He told me he was out of the flat, so he should have been here by now. Did something happen along the way? Did the police catch up with him somehow?

Or has he done a runner with all the money?

It's the last possibility that I deem to be the most likely, and it's the one that causes me to leave my unfinished pint on the table and rush out of the pub and back onto the breezy Promenade.

I almost bump into an old man eating a bag of chips as I hurry down the road with my head buried in my mobile phone, typing out a message to my partner as I go.

"I hope you're not doing something you'll regret?"

I press Send but keep the phone in my hand as I walk, hoping that I'll receive a message straight back any second now that will put my doubts to bed and have me scurrying back to the pub after learning this was all a misunderstanding. But the fact my phone doesn't vibrate with any incoming messages keeps me headed away from the pub and in the direction of the flat at the corner of Jossels Road.

I recognise the grimy brown door from the last time I was here and put my hand against the peeling paintwork and knock hard three times. I'm not expecting James to be in this flat, but I'm hoping the woman who he was living with is. Her name is Christine, and James has been staying here with her after he got out of prison. She's an ex-girlfriend of his from before he served time, but he was using her more as a free place to crash rather than to try to rekindle any past romance between them. It was at this flat a couple of weeks ago where I met James after my own release, and he told me about the teenager he had met online and the safe she knew of in her mother's bedroom. Back then, this flat had been the place where our exciting master plan had been formed. But now I fear it may be the place where it all comes crashing down.

I'm just about to knock again on the ramshackle door when it suddenly swings open, and I see Christine standing there in her dressing gown. She looks like she's just woken up, and maybe she has. James told me she worked nights at the casino down by the seafront. *What a life.* Spending all night serving drinks to the degenerate gamblers of this poxy seaside town and all day sleeping it off in this grimy flat that looks like it should be knocked down. But she isn't my problem right now. The man she had allowed into her home is.

'Have you seen James?' I ask, cutting past all the pleasantries because there simply isn't time for any.

'I was hoping that it was him knocking,' Christine replies, rubbing her bleary eyes and looking past me down the street as if she wasn't aware that daylight was a thing. 'You know you just woke me up. I've got work tonight.'

'Do you know where he might be?' I ask, my tone growing more desperate by the minute. 'It's really important that I speak to him.'

'I've no idea. I saw him this morning when I got back from work, but I've been asleep since then. He isn't up here now.'

'You must have some idea. He lives with you!'

'Just call him,' Christine replies with a shrug, and

she goes to close the door, but I put out my hand to stop it.

'He's not picking it up. Can I come in and have a look around for anything that might tell me where he might be?'

'No, you can't,' Christine replies curtly, and she tries to close the door again.

But I'm getting seriously pissed off now, and this woman isn't helping me, so I barge my way past her and head up the stairs.

'Hey! What are you doing?' Christine calls after me, but I ignore her and enter the door at the top of the stairs that takes me into her home, if you can even call it that. There's a mattress on the floor, several open bin bags of clothes that the occupier hasn't unpacked, and an empty pizza box lying on the grotty kitchen counter. But one thing concerns me amongst the mess, and it's something that's missing that was definitely here the last time I visited.

'Where are his things?' I ask Christine as she reaches the top of the stairs, looking like she is about to hit me.

'What?' she replies, but her anger quickly evaporates when she notices what I already have.

There is nothing here that belongs to James. It's hard to tell amongst all the mess, but the more I look, the more I see.

James has cleaned his stuff out.

'I don't understand. His things were here this morning,' Christine says, scratching her head.

'He must have cleared out while you were asleep.'

'The cheeky bastard,' Christine mutters as she realises he has done a runner on her, but there's no way she can be feeling as hard done by as I am right now.

'Is there anything here that is his?' I ask, hoping for a

small glimmer of hope as I search the tiny flat, but Christine just shakes her head.

'This is all mine,' she replies, clearly upset about James's sudden disappearance.

I bet she thought he was the only woman she was seeing too.

'There has to be something here,' I say, more out of desperation than of any real belief. I can't believe my partner would have screwed me over like this. Without me and what I did on that train, he never would have got the code to that safe. I'll kill him if I ever get my hands on him again. But first, I need to figure out how I might be able to do that.

'There's got to be something he left behind,' I say, rummaging through the bin bags of clothes.

'Hey, those are my things!' Christine protests, and unfortunately, she is right.

I let out a cry of frustration and kick the nearest bin bag to me, expecting it to be full of yet more of the homeowner's clothes. But instead, it's a rubbish bag, and the top bursts open, spilling the contents out across the floor.

'Hey!' Christine cries again, and I'm just about to storm out when I see the piece of paper lying amongst the empty beer cans and microwave meal wrappers.

I scoop it up and open it out to see James's handwriting scrawled across it. I recognise it from the crosswords he would do when we were in prison to pass the time. He's written out a series of times, but I'm not sure what they relate to.

18:42
18:59
19:12
19:27

My eyes scan down the list, trying to figure out what they might be. But then I see the final entry and I know. These are train times. I know that because of the underlined words written beside the last entry.

21:12 – last Eurostar of the day.

41

AMANDA

I didn't expect to be back on a train again so quickly considering how eventful my last journey was, but here I am. The countryside is whizzing by my window, and my elbows are leaning against the table as the carriage shakes all around me. But unlike the last time I was on a train, I actually have hope. That's because I'm no longer the prey.

This time, I'm the hunter.

'Why is it not updating?' I ask my daughter sitting beside me as we stare at the laptop screen on the table in front of us.

'He must be on the tube,' she replies as she continues to refresh the page. 'There's no signal down there, so it won't update until he's out.'

'Okay,' I reply, trying to stay positive. That makes sense. The signal from the phone will come back as soon as he goes above ground again, and all we can do until then is remain patient. The problem is that isn't an easy thing to do when there's so much at stake.

But I console myself with the knowledge that we have been able to track Louise's mobile phone this far, so there's no reason to think that we won't be able to for a little longer yet. Unless James throws it away, of course. *Then we are screwed.* But neither of us want to dwell on the negatives right now. We have to believe that we are going to be able to find James again using this technology, and when we do, I will be able to get back what he stole from my safe.

Ever since Louise told me there was a way to see where her mobile phone was, we have been keeping an eye on the red dot as it has moved around the south of England. When we first saw it, it was already heading north out of Brighton, and the speed of its movement suggested to me that James was on a train. After a frantic few minutes to get ready and prepare myself mentally, Louise and I took a taxi to the train station and purchased a couple of tickets to London to give chase. While we couldn't be sure that London was his destination, we figured it was as good a guess as any considering the direction he was headed, so we decided to start making our own way north so the gap between us and that red dot didn't grow any bigger.

It had been ten minutes since we saw that the red dot was at London Victoria Station, which gave us hope that James's journey was coming to an end and we could catch him up. But then the signal went dead, and we are left refreshing the page, praying that it will pop back up again when he emerges from the tube, if that is what has caused us to lose track of him for now.

'Come on, where are you?' Louise mutters under her breath as she double taps the mouse pad again. Even though the circumstances are far from ideal, I feel glad that she and I are spending some time together. At first, I was completely against the idea of Louise joining me as I went after James, not willing to risk her being in any more danger than she has already been in today. But she insisted on coming, and after all she has been through because of me, I could hardly say no. Besides, she seems to understand this technology on her laptop much better than I do, and the fact she is accessing the internet through something called a dongle is just more evidence of that. It helps to have her operating the laptop while I stare out of the window and think about what I will do if and when I am able to catch up with the man who stole from me.

I have a plan, one that Louise helped me put together, but it isn't without risk, and I'm not confident of its chance of success. But it's the best one we could come up with in the limited time we had before we raced from the flat to the station, and we at least have this train journey to London to iron out the details.

"It's so weird seeing you as a blonde,' Louise says with an amused look on her face. I smile, which may be the first time I've done that since I realised the man on the train wasn't flirting with me earlier. 'I might have to borrow it for a night out sometime.'

'You're not old enough for a night out,' I remind my daughter with a wry smile.

She is referring to the wig I put over my dark hair before leaving the flat, which, along with my change of clothes and dark sunglasses, is part of the disguise I am wearing tonight for my potential encounter with James. It's a similar disguise to the one that I wore for my escorting jobs, although this time I'm not wearing it just because I'm worried about male clients trying to find me online after our dates.

I'm wearing it because it's my only way of getting close enough to James without him realising that something is wrong.

I figured that James would most likely be aware of my appearance, either through his work with his partner as they followed me over the last few weeks or simply because he saw the photos of me around my flat when he visited Louise. Therefore, a disguise is in order if I want to get close to him without raising his suspicions. The plan Louise and I have come up with requires me to get very close to the thief, but I'm confident that my trusty escorting disguise and persona is going to help me do just that. The fact that my own daughter barely recognised me when I emerged from the bathroom after getting changed told me all I needed to know about how good a disguise it actually is. But that doesn't mean it's a comfortable one.

'I hate this thing,' I say as I fiddle with the wig for what must be the hundredth time since we boarded the train. 'It's so itchy.'

'But you look hot,' Louise says with a shrug, as if that is more important than comfort, which perhaps it is. 'No wonder you made so much as an escort. Maybe I should give it a go.'

'Don't even think about it,' I reply with a stern expression.

'Well, hopefully, neither of us will have to do that after tonight,' she says as she goes back to refreshing her laptop. 'Aha!' she cries suddenly. 'I've got him! He's at King's Cross.'

My daughter was right. James must have been on the tube. That explains how he got across the city so quickly.

'Where do you think he is going?' I ask again, even though there is no way for either of us to really know until we catch up with him.

'I'm not sure. From King's Cross, he could get a train to pretty much anywhere in the UK,' Louise replies, and I'm afraid she is right.

I wonder just how far from Brighton we are going to

have to go tonight to try to catch him. But it doesn't matter. I'll go to the ends of the Earth to get back the things from my safe if I have to.

'Unless…' Louise says, thinking out loud.

'What?'

'Well, it's not just trains to parts of the UK that go from there,' Louise says, and a wave of nausea comes over me as I realise that she is right. St Pancras Station is right beside King's Cross, and from that particular station, he could get a train into Europe.

'The Eurostar,' I say dejectedly.

Louise nods.

'Will we be able to track him on this if he goes abroad?' I ask my daughter.

'I'm not sure. I don't know if it works overseas.'

'Shit,' I say, because that's about the best word to sum up the situation right now.

I turn to look back out of the window, silently cursing this train driver and the speed at which we are going. We're going fast, of course, but it isn't quick enough, especially not if the man we are chasing is preparing to board a train out of the country.

'We're going to get him, Mum,' Louise says to me after a moment of silence between us.

'Yeah,' I reply, nodding my head, more for her benefit than my own. 'We're going to get him.'

But I don't feel any better for saying it. That's because after all the bad luck I have had in my life, I don't believe a single word of it.

42

I hate waiting. I feel as if it's what I've spent most of my day doing so far. Waiting for the right time to call around at Louise's flat. Waiting for the safe code. And now finally, waiting for the train that will take me out of England and help me leave behind the women I stole from and the partner I screwed over in the process.

I just want to get moving. I hate inaction. But there is still twenty minutes until the Eurostar is due to depart, so for the time being, I'm stuck here in this departures lounge with the rest of the passengers who are waiting to go to Amsterdam.

It's not that I'm nervous about being caught before I can flee the country. My chances of being stopped now are slim, mainly because I'm moving so fast that I'll be long gone before anyone can catch up with me. I suspect my partner is still sitting in that pub on the Brighton seafront, and while he has surely figured out by now that he has been double-crossed, he will have no idea where I am and how to stop me. Our plan was to board the Eurostar to Paris tomorrow morning, so perhaps he thinks he will be able to catch me at this station then. But he'll be disappointed when he doesn't see me here because I'll be long gone by then.

Looking down at the rucksack by my feet, I long to unzip it and take another look at the contents. All that money just waiting to be spent. I'm going to have some serious fun with it soon, but this is not the time to draw any attention to myself. Right now, I just need to look like a normal English tourist heading to Holland for some fun.

I glance up at the screen above my head to double-check that the service is still running on time, which it is, before I plan to close my eyes and have a moment's rest after what has been an eventful day. But the vibration from my mobile phone in my pocket disrupts me, and I take it out to see that it's my partner calling me again. He's already tried me several times, as well as having sent me a series of text messages, but they have all gone unanswered, just like this one will. I'm tempted to just turn my phone off, but then he will know for sure that I've screwed him—leaving it on at least makes it plausible that I'm currently distracted and unable to get back to him. The longer he is uncertain about what I have done to him, the better, and the text message that flashes up on my phone now confirms that he still has no idea what I am up to.

"Where are you? I'm getting worried. Can you still make it to the pub?"

I smile at my partner's naivete and feel tempted to text back that I'm on my way. But I don't want to play with him too much. The poor man will be suffering enough once he learns that all his hard work following Amanda over the last weeks has gone to waste, as well as everything that he went through on that train with her today. But I don't feel bad for him. Not one bit.

That's because I know he can be equally as ruthless as I am being right now. I learnt that in prison when I watched him stand by as a fellow inmate whom he called a friend was beaten by several other prisoners, and he did nothing to step in and help. There is a cold streak beneath that slick persona of his, and I have no doubt that he would have looked to screw me over at the first opportunity at some point in the future if I didn't get in there first.

Nor do I feel sorry for Christine, my ex-girlfriend, who kindly offered me a place to stay upon my release from prison, only for me to ditch her and disappear while she slept. She's not a bad person, but she's hardly a winner, and I can't hope to go far in life taking somebody like her along for the ride. That's why I sneaked out of her flat this afternoon while she was asleep, stuffing the few belongings I had into my rucksack and heading round to Louise's to put the plan into action. Christine has probably woken up by now and realised that my stuff has gone, and she probably feels hurt that I used her, but she'll get over it, just like my partner will. Besides, she's no saint either. I know she's been stealing money from that casino she works at, and the only reason I didn't try to get a piece of that action was because the potential profit was too small. She's happy skimming a few pounds here and there from her employers, but I need so much more than that to make it worth my time. That's why she's still stuck in that grotty flat in Brighton with a few pounds to her name, and I'm about to board a train to Amsterdam with thousands of pounds to mine.

That just leaves Louise as the other person I have betrayed today. Unlike my partner and Christine, as far as I know, she has never been guilty of a crime and so probably doesn't deserve what I have done to her and her mother. She's just a typical teenager, unsure of her path in life and thinking that every guy that shows an interest in her is doing so because he loves her. I'll have taught her several important lessons today, the most important one of which is that she shouldn't trust anybody, and that even extends to her mother, who clearly had way more money saved in that safe than she had been letting on.

What does Amanda think about what has happened today? Does she blame me and my partner for undoing all her hard work in saving that money? Does she blame her daughter for giving me this opportunity to steal from her? Or does she just blame herself for not being strong enough to keep the code to that safe a secret, even if it cost her daughter her life?

I guess I'll never know. But one thing is for sure.

Amanda is just as pathetic as the rest of them.

43

It's a relief to be out of the tunnels of the London Underground and back in the fresh air again and not just because it was so crowded down there. It's because Louise is able to get a Wi-Fi connection again now that we are above ground, and that means we are able to check on James's location.

After a brief moment of holding my breath while the laptop screen refreshes, I see the red dot again. Louise's phone is still at this station.

That means James is here.

But that doesn't mean it's going to be easy to find him. King's Cross and St Pancras are two of the busiest stations in the country. There are thousands of people rushing all around us right now, going in and out of the station.

Commuters. Tourists. Locals.

So many faces.

How are we ever going to find the one we need?

'Is there any way of narrowing it down a little?' I ask Louise as she holds the laptop in front of her and tries to get a more precise location on her phone.

'I think this is as good as it gets,' she replies. 'My phone is definitely in the station somewhere, but it's not accurate enough to show me the exact place.'

I scratch my itchy scalp again beneath the wig as I look around at the crowds of people swarming past us. A needle in a haystack is the only way to describe the task facing us now.

'Let's check the Eurostar first,' I decide, heading towards the section of the bustling station. 'If we're wrong, then at least it means he is only going somewhere in the UK.'

I know the way because I'd taken the Eurostar once before on a work trip to Brussels two years ago. Our boss took us all away to celebrate a big contract the company had been awarded, and we had a great three days in the Belgian city. I distinctly remember being pretty tipsy before the train even left London on its way into Europe, but it's safe to say my mood is decidedly less upbeat as I return to that same scene.

Louise continues to check her laptop as we walk, and it's a minor miracle that she hasn't dropped it yet amidst all the pushing and shoving that we are having to contend with as we make our way through the heaving station. We finally reach the entrance to the Eurostar, and that's where my daughter tells me that she thinks the red dot is located somewhere close by. That gives me hope, but the long lines of passengers standing in front of the ticket desks do not. This part of St Pancras looks more like an airport than a train station, with check-in areas and large screens with the words 'International Departures' emblazoned across them, and it's almost as busy as one too.

'Can you see him anywhere?' I ask my daughter desperately, feeling overwhelmed by the size of the task ahead of us.

'No,' she replies, her eyes scanning the crowd. 'But he has to be here somewhere. My phone is close by.'

I look at the rows of check-in desks and realise I'm going to have to make a gamble.

'I'm going to buy a ticket and go in. He must be on the other side,' I say, reaching into my handbag for my purse and passport. Fortunately, while my safe might have been emptied, I still have my credit card and passport on me. I carry that important document everywhere with me in case I ever need ID because I don't drive, and not having a driving licence means it's often the only thing I can use to verify my identity.

'How do you know where he is going?' Louise asks me.

'It doesn't matter. I just need to get through security, and I'll hopefully find him in the lounge.'

'Yeah, but you still have to buy a ticket. You should try to get the right train just in case you have to get on it to follow him.'

'I'm not going to Europe and leaving you behind,' I tell my daughter, and I mean it, but she doesn't seem so sure.

'You might have to,' she tells me. 'If that's what it takes to get the things back.'

I realise she might be right so look up at the large electronic screen for the upcoming departures. The next train is to Paris. The one after that is Amsterdam. Then it's Brussels.

'I guess I'll pick Paris,' I say, shrugging my shoulders.

'Wait,' Louise says, and I notice she is also looking up at the screen too. 'Try Amsterdam.'

'Why?' I ask.

'That was one of the places James told me he wanted to go,' she says, and I notice the look of sorrow flash across her face. In all the craziness of today, I had almost forgotten that Louise wasn't just dealing with a threat to her life—she was also dealing with a broken heart after the man she trusted betrayed her. I know exactly how it feels to have such a thing happen, which means I understand how much she must be hurting now.

'I'm sorry about what he did to you, Lou,' I say, shaking my head. 'And I'm sorry that you didn't feel like you could tell me you were seeing somebody.'

'You wouldn't have approved,' she says with a weak smile.

'Maybe so, but from now on, no more secrets, okay?'

Louise nods. 'No more secrets.'

With that, I refocus on the task at hand and make one final check on the laptop screen for the current location of Louise's phone.

'You stay on this side in case the red dot moves away,' I tell my daughter. 'If not, then he is through here, and I'll find him.'

'Okay,' Louise agrees, looking nervous enough for the both of us.

'Can I see the photo again?' I say to her just before I leave, and she opens the folder on her laptop that shows me the image of James she has saved to her device. She told me that she snapped the photo of him while he was sleeping in her bed a few weeks ago, and I'm glad she did because without it I would have no choice but to take my daughter with me to identify him. Thankfully, I can leave Louise here now, meaning she will be nowhere near the dangerous events that are about to take place.

'Got it,' I say, confident that I have memorised the appearance of the man I am looking for. Then I go to head towards the check-in desk, but Louise grabs my arm just before I can leave.

'Be careful,' she tells me, and I smile because despite all the arguments and ordeals we have been through together, she still cares about me. Maybe things never had to be so bad between us in the first place.

'I always am,' I reply, squeezing her hand before rushing to join the shortest queue I can find at the departure desk.

Once in place, I glance back over my shoulder at where Louise is waiting for me, and hope this won't be the last time I ever see her. But I know I'm potentially heading into a very dangerous situation, and I can't predict the outcome, even though I have a plan. The truth is that if James was clever enough to get his hands on the contents of my safe, he may be clever enough to get out of what I am planning to do to him, and if he does, then there's no telling what might happen.

I'm desperate to get my belongings back.

He'll be desperate to keep them.

But only one of us is going to get our way.

A few minutes later, I'm at the front of the queue, and as I watch the couple in front of me take their tickets from the clerk behind the desk and walk away, it's now my turn to step forward from the line.

I decide to ask for a ticket to Amsterdam based on Louise's prediction, but it doesn't really matter if I'm right or wrong about where James is going. I just need to get to the lounge past this point.

I hand my credit card and passport over to the female clerk before remembering to lift up my sunglasses as she checks my photo.

I want her to be able to recognise me, even with a change in hair colour.

It's only James I need to deceive now.

44

JAMES

'Now boarding London to Amsterdam. Please proceed to platform two.'

The sound of the female voice over the tannoy is like music to my ears, and I pick up my heavy rucksack before joining the other passengers who will be on board this evening service to the Dutch capital. I'm looking forward to getting on and finding my seat, and I'm pleased to see that it's not going to be too busy on board, as most of the people in this departure lounge have remained seated, so they must be headed to Brussels on the next train instead. With a bit of luck, there'll be nobody seated at my table, and I'll be able to put my feet up on the opposing chair. I deserve to travel in comfort after everything I've been through to get to this point.

I leave the departure lounge and head for the ticket barriers, my mind already on the can of lager that I will be purchasing from the drinks trolley on board as soon as we set off. I wonder if my partner has enjoyed his drinks at the pub in Brighton tonight while he waits for me to show up. Something tells me he has not, and another check on my phone indicates that the calls and text messages are still incoming.

"Where are you?"

"Don't tell me you've done a runner."

"I'll kill you if I get my hands on you."

How charming.

And he wonders why I haven't bothered to text him back.

I'm just about to turn my phone off when I hear the sound of a suitcase clattering to the floor behind me, and I turn around to see a pretty redhead struggling to pick it back up again.

'Let me help you with that,' I say, and the woman thanks me in a distinct Dutch accent.

'Are you from Amsterdam?' I ask her as we continue to make our way towards the ticket barrier, and she tells me that she is.

'Great! I need a tour guide to show me around,' I say cheekily, and I'm pleased to see that she smiles at the joke.

As she slots her ticket into the machine and steps through the barriers onto the other side, I think about how nice it would be to enjoy the company of a proper woman after spending the last few weeks dealing with Louise and her teenage tantrums. Even before I revealed to her what my true intentions were today, she was always wanting to know if I was seeing other women as well as her. But something tells me this lively redhead in front of me wouldn't care about something like that, and I'm eager to get on board and get to know her more. I'm just about to follow her through the barrier and ask her which carriage she is seated in when a tall man cuts in front of me, puts his hand around her waist and apologises for being late.

Damn. She's already taken.

Oh well, I guess I'll be spending the journey alone.

No bother.

A quiet and peaceful trip it is, then.

45

I move quickly through the departure lounge, my head swivelling as I look in all directions for any sign of James. The voice over the tannoy tells me that the next train is leaving in five minutes, so it doesn't give me long to locate him if he is on that one before I risk losing him forever. But so far, I can't see him, and I'm aware that time is running out.

Convinced that he definitely isn't in the lounge, I step out through the doors and head towards the platforms, my eyes firmly on the swarm of people pushing their way through the ticket barriers up ahead. There are dozens of passengers on the other side of the barriers, making their way to the various platforms, where some trains are already waiting, and some are yet to arrive. But if I didn't see James behind me, that means he must be ahead, so I rush towards the barriers with my ticket in hand and slot it into the machine.

I head in the direction of the platform for the Amsterdam service, and I can already see the train is parked with its doors open and ready to take on new passengers, so I'm about to break into a run when I catch sight of a dark-haired man on an opposing platform.

I see the man walking away with his back to me, his head bowed and a rucksack on his shoulder. Is that him? Based on the photo Louise showed me, it certainly could be.

Following the man, I do my best to fight the voice in my head telling me to turn around and go back to my daughter, begging me not to risk my health by going ahead with the plan. But I ignore it and keep running, and I'm about to reach him when he suddenly turns around.

That's when I see that it isn't him.

'Shit,' I say as I watch the man step on board a service to Brussels, annoyed at myself for wasting precious seconds in the pursuit of the wrong person.

Feeling panicked now that time is almost up, I turn around and go to head back down the platform when I feel a tight squeeze on my left arm, and a hand pulls me to the side.

I freeze, wondering if it is James.

Did he spot me while I was trying to spot him?

But then I get a look at the man's face beside me and see that it isn't James.

It's his partner in crime.

'Hello, Amanda,' he says in that sickeningly calm voice of his, and all the fears and anxieties of the day come flooding back to me now that I am with this man again. 'Nice disguise. But I'd recognise that hurried walk of yours anywhere after these last few weeks.'

I try to break free of his grip, but he doesn't allow it as he leads me away from the passengers to a quieter end of the platform.

'Get off me!' I tell him, but I make sure to keep my voice low so as not to draw any attention to our section of the platform. I came here to stop James, but it's obvious I'm going to have to stop his partner too.

'What are you doing here, Amanda? Do you know where he is?'

'What?'

'It turns out you're not the only one who has been screwed today,' he says to me. 'Where is he?'

'What are you talking about?' I ask as he leads me ever closer to the edge of the train platform, and I see the grimy tracks come into view beneath me.

'James! Tell me where he is!'

'I don't know!' I cry, starting to fear that I am going to be thrown down onto the tracks if I don't give him the answer he wants.

'I know he is here somewhere! I know he's getting the Eurostar! Tell me where he is!'

'I don't know!'

That's when I notice the train coming into the station further along the track from where we are now.

I desperately try to break free again, but my captor won't let me go.

I'm going to lose James if I can't lose this man.

So I stop pulling and start pushing instead.

His eyes go wide with fear as he realises what I'm doing, and he loses his grip on me as well as his balance, toppling backwards over the edge of the platform. The power I generated from the shove to his chest sends him down onto the tracks below just as the train arrives.

I almost regret what I have done in that instant and reach out for his hand as it falls away from me, but it's too late. There is a high-pitched squealing of brakes as the train driver does his best to avoid the man who has fallen right in front of his vehicle, but it's no good. An awful sound emerges from beneath the train as it runs over the body, and I turn away as blood splatters up from the tracks, closing my eyes but wishing I had covered my ears too to drown out the horrors behind me.

Somebody screams. Another person shouts. I hear an alarm sound on the train. Panicked voices. Rushing passengers trying to lend aid to the man under the train even though it is obviously too late.

It's chaos, and it's only going to get worse. Soon this part of the station will be overrun with police officers and paramedics.

I need to make sure I'm not here when it is.

As all hell breaks loose around me, I go against the tide of people and rush away from the scene, making my way back along the platform and past the dozens of passengers who are now all gawking at the deadly incident behind me. I keep my head down as I go, praying that nobody tries to stop me and hold me accountable for what just happened. With my disguise, I could get away with this, but only if I'm not caught at the station when the police arrive and check the CCTV. But I can't go anywhere until I have found James.

I haven't come this far to run away now.

I return to the ticket barriers, where I can get a better view of all the other platforms, and I look for any sign of the dark-haired man with the rucksack. The fact that his partner was here too only confirms that James must be at this station. I feel like I'm so close to finding him, but there's just too many people around for me to pick him out.

I turn around and look the other way, ignoring the passengers who are now trying to see why several station employees are running down one of the platforms towards the train that has stopped halfway down the tracks. I'm looking for the one passenger who isn't stopping. The one who isn't distracted. The one who is desperate to get away.

And then I see him.

Over the head of a tall man and a redheaded woman with a large suitcase.

It's James.

I set off in pursuit, running after him, terrified of losing him again now in the crowd after finally finding him. I can see the rucksack slung over his shoulder, and knowing exactly what he has got in there only causes me to quicken my pace.

As I push past a young guy trying to film the chaos in the station on his camera phone, I hear the tannoy click on overhead, and a male voice booms out of the speakers, telling passengers to leave platform five and return to the ticket barriers. But most people here ignore the instruction and continue trying to get a better look at the body on the tracks, their morbid curiosity getting the better of their common sense and respect for the dead.

But I ignore the call from the tannoy too and so does James. I watch as he bends down and scoops up a free newspaper from an unmanned stand before stepping through the doors and boarding the train on platform two.

I stop running now that my chances of losing him have reduced, and instead, I take a moment for my heart rate to settle and my breathing to return to normal. Checking my reflection in the window of the carriage, I make sure that my disguise is still firmly in place.

Then I board the train.

46

This service looks to be a quiet one tonight, and there are plenty of vacant seats as I make my way past them before settling on the one with the table at the end of the carriage.

I've brushed off the disappointment of finding out that the redhead on the platform was not as single as I'd hoped, and now I'm just looking forward to a chilled journey into Holland. There'll be plenty of time for enjoying female company in Amsterdam, I'm sure.

Stuffing the ticket back into my pocket, I slump down into my seat and relieve myself of the heavy weight on my shoulder. I'm grateful for the bag of cash, but I'm ready for a break from lugging it around.

Now where's that drinks trolley?

I look down the carriage but see only a couple more passengers getting on and putting their luggage into the overhead compartments. With no sign of refreshments being on the way yet, I decide to pass the time by flicking through the newspaper I picked up just before I boarded.

I browse through the sports section first before

turning to the front of the paper and thumbing through the current affairs stories. I read so many newspapers in prison, mainly because it was one of the few things to do to pass the time, and I lost count of how many crosswords I completed. I'm just about to go in search of a new one when I notice the news story on page eleven.

MYSTERY AROUND MURDERED DIRECTOR REMAINS UNSOLVED ONE MONTH ON

But it's not the eye-catching headline that grabs my attention. It's the name in the article.

Charles Montague.

I take the ring out and double-check the name engraved on it with the name of the murder victim in the paper.

Charles & Mary Montague 23.05.70

Well, well, well. I guess there were more secrets in that safe than just the money.

Was Amanda related to this dead director? Is this her inheritance? Or did she kill this guy in the paper? Is she the one the police are looking for?

If so, we really had no idea who we were dealing with after all.

I shake my head in disbelief at my discovery. On one hand, this ring is potentially even more valuable than I realised if it belonged to a famous theatre director. But on the other, I'm carrying an item of jewellery belonging to a murder victim.

How would it look if I got caught with this?

It makes sense to me now why it took Amanda so long to give up the code. She wasn't doing it to protect the money. She was doing it to protect her secret. If she obtained this ring illicitly, then it's no surprise that she fought so hard to keep it locked away.

I close the newspaper and toss it onto the empty seat opposite me before taking another look at the ring. I can't believe Louise's mum is such a badass. I'm impressed. But I guess she isn't as bad as me. I'm the one sitting here with all her things, after all.

I place the ring down on the table in front of me and take out my phone, deciding to see if I can get an idea of the valuation on this item of jewellery on the internet. As I do, I'm pleased to see that there have been no calls or messages from my partner in the last ten minutes. I guess after finally figuring out what I have done, he knows there is nothing he can do to catch me now.

I'm just about to Google 'ring valuations' when a blonde woman in dark sunglasses arrives at my table and smiles at me.

'Is it okay if I borrow this newspaper?' she asks, and I shrug.

'Go for it,' I say, returning my gaze to my phone.

The woman picks up the newspaper, and I expect her to continue to make her way to one of the many other empty seats in the carriage, but instead, she sits down opposite me at this table.

'You don't mind, do you?' she says, and while I initially do, I realise it may not be such a bad thing after all.

So what if I had no luck with the redhead.

Maybe that's because I was supposed to meet this blonde.

I smile at the woman as she settles into her seat, noticing that she is attractive from what I can see of her face behind the sunglasses. I'm surprised she hasn't removed them yet, but I'm guessing she is wearing them to make a fashion statement rather than because it's particularly bright on this train. She looks to be much older than me, closer to forty, but that doesn't have to be a bad thing. After the last few weeks with a younger woman, maybe an older one is just what I need.

I decide to put my phone back into my pocket, figuring there will be plenty of time to try to get the ring valued when I get to Amsterdam. For now, I'll try my luck with this pretty passenger opposite me. But before I initiate a conversation, I go to return the ring to my pocket.

That's when the woman compliments me on it and asks if she can have a closer look.

I'm obviously reluctant to hand it over considering I now know what it relates to, so I need to reject her question but in a way that still makes me look good.

'I'm sorry,' I say, putting the precious ring on my finger. 'It's very valuable, and I worry when it's in somebody else's hands. Even ones as dainty as yours.'

47

I'm disappointed that James didn't just hand me the ring, but I always knew it wasn't going to be as easy as that. He looks so smug sitting there with it on his hand, and I'm sure he is looking forward to pawning it as soon as he gets to Amsterdam. But that won't be happening now, nor will he be getting to spend any of the money that I know is packed into that rucksack on the seat beside him.

Now that I have found these things again, it's time to end this, once and for all.

'I understand,' I reply, maintaining my pleasant demeanour. 'It really is a beautiful ring.'

'Thanks,' he says, fiddling with it a little before turning the conversation back onto me.

'So what takes you to Amsterdam?' he asks while very deliberately using his ring hand to scratch his stubble, and I wonder if he is flashing the expensive item of jewellery at me on purpose. Is he trying to impress me? If so, then I don't have to worry about him figuring out who I really am.

He obviously doesn't have the slightest idea.

'Pleasure,' I reply, with a smirk, and he seems to like that answer.

'And you?' I ask.

'The same,' he replies.

'Here's to pleasure, then,' I say suggestively, running my fingers through my fake blonde hair.

I wait for the passenger who has just entered our carriage to make her way past our table before I pick up my handbag from the seat beside me and take out the large packet of crisps inside.

'You don't mind if I open these, do you?' I ask him. 'It's just I've been in such a rush all day, I've barely had time to eat.'

'Not at all,' he replies, and I smile again. He certainly wasn't being this pleasant to me a couple of hours ago. Nor was he being this way with my daughter. It's the knowledge of what he has put Louise through today that gives me the encouragement I need to do what I am about to do, guilt-free and conscience clear.

Just as I'm about to open the bag, I notice the commotion on the neighbouring platforms outside the train window. The crowd has grown larger as more and more people try to get a good look at what happened with the man who went under the train, and I know it won't be long until the police are on the scene. I need to be long gone by then, which means I can't afford to waste another second.

I put both my hands on the top of the crisp packet and pull as hard as I can, deliberately tearing the packet open too much and causing the entire contents of the bag to erupt all over both the table and my fellow passenger.

'Oh, my gosh, I'm so sorry!' I say, feigning horror at what I've just done. 'I guess I don't know my own strength!'

James doesn't look to thrilled about what has just happened, but he's a good sport, and he tells me not to worry about it, before doing the exact thing that I was hoping he would do.

He begins to pick up several of the crisps that have fallen onto his clothes and his rucksack, directly bringing them into contact with his skin.

I tidy up the crisps on the table at the same time for show, but I'm now just waiting for the real show to begin. I wonder how long it will take. Louise told me that it would be fast. Within seconds, she said. Was she exaggerating? Or was she right?

Ten seconds later, I get my answer.

A worried look suddenly flashes across James's face, and he puts his hand to his throat, looking up at me with fear in his eyes.

'Are you okay?' I ask him, doing my best to pretend like I genuinely give a damn.

But he doesn't give me an answer. He doesn't have to. His red face says it all.

'What is in those crisps?' he asks me as he begins to grow more panicked by the second.

'What do you mean?'

'The crisps? Do they have peanuts in?'

I pull my face and play dumb, stalling for time because I know James is short of it now.

'These? I'm not sure,' I say, making a big point of checking the back of the packet for the ingredients. 'I don't think so.'

But James doesn't seem convinced, and I expect him to tell me that they must do, except he says nothing and just focuses on trying to get some air into his lungs.

I guess it's tough to hold a conversation when you're struggling to breathe.

'What's the matter?' I ask him, playing the role of the

concerned stranger in case anybody else in this carriage has noticed what is going on at this table.

'I'm allergic to peanuts,' he gasps as he holds his throat and goes to get up out of his seat.

'Oh, my God, I think they do have peanuts in!' I cry, and I immediately get up out of my own seat and rush to his aid.

I put my hand on his shoulder, and while to an observer it would look like I am trying to help him, I'm really just pushing him back down into the seat to make sure he can't get off this train and seek help.

'In my jacket pocket,' he says, and I see him fumbling to take something out.

It's an EpiPen, the only thing now that could save him.

'You're going to be okay,' I tell him as I take the injectable device from him though I have no intention of using it. Instead, I slip it into my handbag before taking him by the hand and giving it a squeeze to show him my support.

As he continues to struggle for breath, I use my free hand to take out my phone.

'I'll call for help,' I say, and he nods his head desperately, clearly aware that he isn't going to last long without medical assistance. But really, I'm just doing this to kill a few more precious seconds, seconds that I know are vital to his chances of survival.

As I hold the phone to my ear, I use my other hand to slide the ring off his finger, and that's when he realises that I might not be as friendly as he thought.

The grin on my face confirms it.

Lowering the phone and dropping it into my handbag along with the ring, he now knows that I'm not trying to help him at all.

'This is for Louise,' I say, leaning over him and whispering into his ear as he chokes to death. 'And this is for me.'

I pick up the rucksack from the seat beside him and sling it over my shoulder before grabbing my handbag and heading for the door. But before I leave, I take one last look at James as he takes his last few breaths at the table.

His eyes are red and swollen, but I know he sees the smile on my face right before I step off the train and onto the platform.

Once out of the carriage, I vanish from his sight amongst the hordes of passengers here who will keep me well concealed as I make my way out of this station and to somewhere safer where I can get changed out of my disguise. I know I'm running purely on adrenaline right now, and the enormity of what has happened will hit me soon, but I need to be far away from here before then. The police are going to be looking for me shortly once they check the surveillance footage from both the platform where I pushed the man and the train where I put James into anaphylactic shock, so I'd better make sure I don't look anything like this for too much longer. But I'll be sad to take off this wig because it's served me well over the last half an hour.

I guess it's true what they say.

Blondes really do have more fun.

48

AMANDA

THREE MONTHS LATER

I find myself staring out of the window a lot these days. At first, I put it down to the fact that I'm a full-time writer now, so daydreaming is just a part of the job. But then I realised it had nothing to do with seeking inspiration from the outside world, and had more to do with the fact that I've never actually had a decent view to enjoy in the past. All my previous homes have either looked out onto a dreary street or a brick wall, so my current home marks quite the change. From where I am now, I can see rolling green hills all the way down to the sea on the horizon. This is definitely a view worth looking out of the window for.

But I didn't rent this cottage in the East Sussex countryside just to gaze longingly at the scenery all day. I did it because it was a quiet place to come to get my book finished, so with that in mind, I turn my head away from the window and back towards the laptop on this desk. These words aren't going to write themselves, and I didn't go through everything that I endured over the last few years just to waste it all being lazy.

Within seconds, my fingers are tapping the keyboard again, and I feel better for it. Not only is this what I'm supposed to be doing, but when I write, I completely forget about the past and the events that led to me being here right now. But only for a moment. As soon as my hands stop typing and my head swivels back to that window beside me, I'm reminded of what I did and who I had to become just to give myself this opportunity.

I thought I'd experienced enough drama for one lifetime after that night in Charles's apartment, but it turned out that was merely a precursor to the events that were to come a month later on the train. But just like the situation with Charles, I ended up being the last one standing. Both James and his partner are dead. Not many people can survive being pushed under a moving train or coming into contact with peanuts when they are severely allergic. Of course, my intention at the time was never to kill those men, just like I never intended to kill Charles. I was merely doing what I needed to do to survive. I only wanted to disable them so I could make my escape and preserve my safety, but in all three cases, the men died.

Do I feel bad about what happened?

Of course.

But would I do it all again if the circumstances were the same?

After many sleepless nights since, I have to say that yes, I would.

I'm not going to regret accidentally killing a man who was trying to rape me, just like I'm not going to regret killing the two men who threatened my life and the life of my daughter. The simple fact is that they would still be alive now if they were good men. All I have ever tried to do is get what I want, but I never did it to the detriment of another human being. Unfortunately, not everybody has that same control. Some people try to get what they want regardless of who they will hurt in the process. Those three men were like that, and the world is a better place now they are no longer in it.

I sit back in my seat and think about how lucky I am to be able to do what I love every day. I no longer commute on a busy train. I no longer have to sit in meetings and pretend to look interested. And I no longer have to put on a wig and pretend to be someone I'm not as I sit across a table from a guy who is paying me to be on a date with him.

All the hard work and sacrifices have been worth it, and while it was a wild and unpredictable ride to get to this point, now I have accomplished my goal. I wake up every day in a lovely cottage in the countryside and write words on a page. It's all I ever wanted to do, and now I get to do it. I even have a publisher interested in reading this book when it's finished.

Oh my.

But perhaps the best thing to come out of this whole thing is not my new career, but my new relationship with my daughter. After years of arguments, door slamming, and disappointment, we are now getting on better than ever. A lot of it has to do with what we went through together on that fateful day three months ago when she was held at knifepoint, and I was blackmailed into opening my safe. I guess no relationship would be the same after something like that. But I think the main thing that the whole experience taught us was that we weren't as different as we thought.

We're both stubborn, and while that led to a lot of arguments in the past, it also led to neither one of us giving up easily in the face of danger that day. We both kept secrets, me with my past and her with her "boyfriend", and we both now know that keeping things from each other is more trouble than it's worth. We're also both dreamers, her with travelling and me with writing, and while that used to be the cause of many disagreements, we can now see that we share that same zest to achieve our goals that so many other people in society lack.

I used to think we argued all the time because we were so different.

But it turned out it's because we are too similar.

Thinking of my daughter now makes me wish I could speak to her, but that isn't an easy thing to do these days. That's because she's currently over six thousand miles away exploring Vietnam while I'm sitting here in this cosy little hideaway in the English countryside. I do miss Louise, but I'm happy she has gone because I know it's what she wants to do. Once the dust had settled after the events at St Pancras Station and I had made it home safely with the money intact, I told my daughter that I would give her the funds to go travelling. To my surprise, she initially refused, telling me that I had made enough sacrifices for her over the years and that money would be better spent pursuing my dreams instead of hers. But as always, I disagreed with my daughter, only this time it didn't lead to an argument. It led to her wrapping her arms around me and declaring me to be the best mum in the world. While I'm not sure I will ever deserve that lofty title, I do know that she is happier now than she has been in a long time, so I must have done something right.

It's been a couple of days since we last spoke, the

wonders of modern technology allowing her to video call me from an internet café in Hanoi and update me on her adventures. She's already been through Thailand, and her next stop is Indonesia, but she somehow managed to find the time in her busy schedule to give me a quick call and tell me that she loves me. The money I gave her is allowing her to see the world, and I know she will return a more grown-up and well-rounded individual. *That's if she returns at all.* She's already talking about the possibility of heading to Australia once she is done exploring Asia, which sounded expensive to me, right up until the moment she told me she had already been looking into how to get a job to fund her stay while she is over there.

My daughter talking about getting a job?

I had to hold on to the desk to stop myself falling over in shock.

But the best thing about seeing my daughter so happy now is that it makes me feel happy too. I'd spent so long focusing on my own goals that I neglected hers, but that dramatic day a couple of months ago gave me a wake-up call and showed me that my daughter and I are a team and not just two clashing opponents.

I think the two men who tried to steal from us would admit that we were more than worthy opponents too, if only they were here to comment.

Checking the clock in the corner of my laptop screen, I decide that it's time for a short break from my workstation. It's important to keep my mind fresh when I'm holed up in here all day with nothing but my overactive imagination to keep me company, and there's no better way to do that than to go outside and get some fresh air. It's a bright and breezy day in this part of the world, and I can't wait to get my boots on and go for a quick stroll around the grounds of this cottage. A short break will do me good before I return to finish my latest chapter and move one step nearer to having a finished manuscript to send the publisher.

But before I go, I make sure to pick up my laptop from the desk and carry it into the bedroom, where I place it carefully on the bed while I open the wardrobe opposite. Then I crouch down and place my finger on the glass panel that sits on the front of the safe, and as it registers my fingerprint, I hear a soft click before the door pops open.

It's not just my lifestyle that has been upgraded recently.

It's my home security too.

I place the laptop inside the safe, as I always do before leaving the cottage, because this is the best way to protect my precious manuscript while I am gone. Of course, I have backed it up on USB sticks and online drives, but they can be lost or hacked, whereas an iron safe that can only be unlocked by my fingerprint is not going to be as easy to access.

With the laptop safely stored away until my return, I'm just about to close the door when I catch sight of the gold band at the back of the safe. It's been a while since I handled it, and I am still meaning to sell it, but for the time being, it remains in my possession, and I pick it up to take another look at it.

I had the engraving on the ring removed in Rome during a little holiday with Louise shortly after the events on the train, so any chance of me being linked back to Charles's murder has gone. All that is left for me to do is pawn it and take the money, but I've found myself hanging onto it for the time being. I think it's because it reminds me of what I did to get to this point, and it's also a reminder of the kind of things I may be forced to do again if I don't make this writing dream work. There's not much better motivation to get words on the page every day than seeing an item that reminds me of so much death, deceit and desperation. I never want to be that woman again, the one who was seen as an easy target for sex and profit by nefarious men. This ring reminds me that I am a new person now, and as long as it stays in this safe, then I can never forget what I went through to keep it here.

I place the ring back inside and close the door before pressing my finger on the keypad again to engage the lock. With the safe secure, I leave the bedroom and put on my boots before opening the door and stepping outside into the bright, warm sunshine. Within minutes, I am away from the cottage and walking along a delightful little stream that cuts through this landscape, and I feel truly at one with nature as I take in all the sights and sounds of this beautiful part of the country. The birds in the trees. The wind in the leaves.

The train in the distance.

I pause and listen to the low rumbling somewhere over the other side of the hill from where I stand. It's the first time I've noticed that sound before out here, but no matter.

It's not enough to spoil my walk.

It's only a train.

I can handle those.

ABOUT THE AUTHOR

Did you enjoy The Passenger? Please consider leaving a review on Amazon to help other readers discover the book.

Daniel Hurst writes psychological thrillers and loves to tell tales about unusual things happening to normal people. He has written all his life, making the progression from handing scribbled stories to his parents as a boy to writing full length novels in his thirties. He lives in the North West of England and when he isn't writing, he is usually watching a game of football in a pub where his wife can't find him.

Want to connect with Daniel? Visit him at his website or on any of these social media channels.

www.danielhurstbooks.com

ALSO BY DANIEL HURST

INKUBATOR TITLES

THE BOYFRIEND
(A Psychological Thriller)

THE PASSENGER
(A Psychological Thriller)

THE PROMOTION
(A Psychological Thriller)

THE NEW FRIENDS
(A Psychological Thriller)

THE BREAK
(A Psychological Thriller)

THE ACCIDENT
(A Psychological Thriller)

THE INTRUDER
(A Psychological Thriller)

Published by Inkubator Books
www.inkubatorbooks.com

Made in the USA
Monee, IL
03 July 2023